The Rose and Crown

The Rose and Crown:
The Cozy Cat Bookstore Mysteries Book 2

This is a work of **fiction**, a product of the author's imagination.
Any resemblance to actual persons, living or dead, or actual
events, is purely coincidental, unless part of the historical record,
with which some liberties may certainly have been taken.

Copyright © 2023 Lisa-Anne Wooldridge

All rights reserved. No part of this book may be
reproduced or used in any manner without the prior
written permission of the copyright owner, except for
the use of brief quotations in a book review.

To request permissions, contact the publisher
at revelarebooks.com

Paperback: 978-1-7373295-2-7
e-book: 978-1-7373295-3-4

Cover Art Copyright © 2022 Ivy Wooldridge, Liz Birdwell

Revelare Books
Cottage Grove, OR

www.revelarebooks.com

The Rose and Crown

Lisa-Anne Wooldridge

To my children

(The ones I got the hard way and the ones I absconded with)

Thank you for sharing your stories with
me and letting me tell you a tale or two.
You are the little protagonists
Andrew and I always dreamed of!

And to Jessica and Mike

Never did an adventurer have a better family
to caravan with through life.
The Wordwell Wagon Train will ride again!

Chapter One

*L*ucy stood back and admired her handiwork. The soft, golden glow of the fairy lights transformed the safari tent into something magical. She'd wrapped the delicate strands around the rough beams and rails framing the canvas structure and then hung a few along the peak edge overhanging the zippered door.

Perhaps it was gilding the lily, considering the tent's interior was beautifully decorated and welcoming. Still, Lucy thought her campsite looked charming and festive with the additions. Inside, the bed had layers of quilts and a down-filled comforter, but the best feature was the heated mattress. She looked forward to slipping into that warm bed, knowing the temperature along the coast would drop after the sun sank below the horizon. Autumn days in California were typically beautiful and warm, but the night air was a different story.

She was one of only a few campers occupying the platform tents scattered throughout the redwood cove. The site had some common areas—a water station and dish-washing sink, a shelter with several barbecue grills, and across the meadow, a welcome center with tea, coffee, and hot chocolate. There were s'mores kits on offer for a small fee, too, but Lucy had packed her own. The bathrooms were indulgent and luxurious, more in keeping with a nice spa than a campground. Beautiful fresh flowers even brightened the sink.

Lucy pulled out her phone and pushed a button on the app that connected her with the host. She chose "campfire valet" from the options and confirmed her site number. She giggled to herself. It wasn't as if she couldn't build her own campfire—because she surely could! She was there as a favor to the new owners to test out the amenities in a soft launch before the grand opening. This was no ordinary campground. It was glamping, and Lucy was sure it would be popular despite the eye-watering prices.

Faster than Lucy could put her phone away, a fresh-faced young man in a staff polo and khaki shorts drove up on a tiny e-cart and unloaded a pile of wood into Lucy's fire pit. He laughed when he noticed the strings of fairy lights Lucy had added to her tent.

"Those are a great idea. I'm going to ask the boss to come take a look if you don't mind?" He gave her a shy smile before splitting a few logs into smaller pieces. "I'm Kevin, by the way."

"Oh, that's fine. I'm just happy to be here," Lucy said. "This place is just stunning, and I can't wait to tell everyone about it. And I'm Lucy. I own, er, co-own the bookstore in town, The Cozy Cat."

"That's what we hope for. And that all our guests will want to return. My aunt and uncle own the place, and I'm just here until Thanksgiving. I need to finish up my last year of college, but the classes I need aren't offered until the spring semester. Is there anything else I can do for you?" The fire was beginning to catch and crackle.

"No. Thanks, Kevin. That's all I needed. I'll be sure to message if anything else comes up." Lucy tried to hand Kevin a tip, but he refused, explaining that they weren't taking tips until after the grand opening.

Other campers had already begun cooking their dinners, some over their own fire pits and others taking advantage of the gas grills. Her stomach growled, so Lucy dug her own dinner out of the small cooler she'd packed. She wished she had someone to share the experience with, but no one had been available. Mark, the Coast Guard captain she'd fallen for several months before, was away on a training mission, and all her other friends were too busy to come.

Lucy was enthralled with watching what patches of sky she could see through the trees turn pink, purple, and gold—as if the trees were strung with jewels before the light faded. As twilight descended, strings of lights high overhead switched on. They lit up various corners of the campground, highlighting the thick tree trunks and cozy tent cabins. The whole place was transformed into something where elves and hobbits would be at home. She heard several people exclaim at the sight, and one little girl in a tent across from Lucy's stood up and clapped. Lucy smiled to herself. *It's no wonder I enjoy kids so much.*

Lucy joined in clapping with the little girl, and soon, several others did too. She could hear a few people laughing and some muted applause from the other end of the campground as the wave of cheers made its way around the sites. A sense of camaraderie came after the cheering ended, and people began introducing themselves to their nearest neighbors. Lucy felt a bit isolated, having no one to share the moment with and no near neighbor on her side of the grove.

She pulled out a pack of hot dogs from her cooler and threaded two onto a double skewer, which she then rested in a notch on the side of the fire pit. She could have used the swinging grate, but hot dogs on a stick were just better in every way. They were the perfect height to cook slowly, all the way through, and not burn on the outside. She'd just put two buns and some ketchup and mustard packets from Hattie's café on the stump seat next to her when visitors from several directions approached her all at once.

They all looked at each other and then at Lucy. *Awkward,* she thought when no one volunteered to speak first. The little girl from across the grove was alone, so Lucy focused on her. "Hello! What's your name?" *Adults can wait,* she thought, *but children shouldn't have to.*

"I'm Emma. I came to thay thankth for clapping with me." Emma was clearly missing a couple of teeth, giving her an adorable lisp.

Lucy stood up and handed Emma a card from her back pocket. "Hi, Emma! I'm so happy to meet you. My name's Lucy, and I own The Cozy Cat Bookstore in town. I don't think I've ever seen you in there, but if you come and ask for me, I'll help you find a book you can take home as a gift. I am so glad you stood up and clapped because this place deserves it!"

"Wow, really? Thankth, Luthy."

One of Lucy's other visitors, a barrel-shaped man in his late fifties, got down on Emma's level. "Oh, it was you who started all that noise?"

Emma's eyes widened, and Lucy took a protective step toward the little girl. Emma didn't say a word but instead looked toward her parents on the other side of the grove. Lucy wondered if the little girl was about to bolt.

The man couldn't keep a straight face. He glanced up at Lucy and then gave Emma a massive smile. "Young lady, thank you for that. I've never had a standing ovation before. I'm so glad you like the campground." He fumbled with something in his wallet. "Tell you what, take this card too, and give it to your parents. Because you are so nice, I'm inviting you to come back and camp with us again—on the house."

Emma tilted her head and stared. Lucy added, "He means for free, Emma. He's the owner of the campground. On the house means for free."

The little girl took the card, "thankthed" him, and ran.

"Lucy, thank you." He handed her a card too. "I'm Ed Klaas. I'd love for you to come back as our guest, as well. I really wasn't sure how well we'd do as a new business here, but with support like this from other business owners in town, I'm not sure we can fail."

"That's not necessary, Ed. I'm just glad to be here now. Thank you for inviting me. This place really is something special. I have no doubt you will succeed. If you want to give me some brochures, I'd be happy to keep them in the bookstore. We do get a fair bit of tourist traffic coming through."

"Please keep it, Lucy. And feel free to bring guests with you too. Besides, I have a favor to ask." He nodded toward the other person he'd brought with him. She was about Lucy's age, with tanned skin and amber eyes. She'd been smiling without speaking the whole time but didn't wait to be introduced now.

"Hi. I'm Graciela, and your hot dogs are about to burn!"

"Oh!" Lucy jumped back to her spot by the fire and turned the skewer over so that the other side now faced the flames. "Thank you! You saved my dinner."

"That was the favor I wanted to ask you, Lucy. Graciela was hesitant to have a fire lit for just herself and wondered if she could share one with someone else. Since you and she are the only two singletons, I was hoping . . . ?"

"I'd love that. No problem at all!" Lucy was a bit relieved. Company sounded good. It would be nice to have someone to talk to around the fire.

"Okay, thanks, Lucy. Graciela, I'll have Kevin bring your cooler over. Is there anything else you want him to grab for you?"

Ed seemed in a hurry to leave now that everything was taken care of.

"Yes, please have him grab my thermos and picnic basket too. Thanks, Ed!" Graciela turned to Lucy as the older man hurried off. "Thanks again. I really didn't look forward to cooking and eating all alone. Oh, and call me Gracie. Everyone does."

"Would you like a hot dog, Gracie?"

Nestled under a thick blanket, Lucy sat by the dying fire. She was full—two hot dogs and half a bag of marshmallows—and mesmerized by the white fire of the stars overhead. Framed by the tips of the giant redwood trees rimming the grove, the usual night sky seemed more like a work of art with glittering diamonds on a deep navy canvas. She and Graciela had immediately hit it off, talking and laughing like old friends for several hours. Once the quiet hours began, Gracie set off for her own tent, leaving Lucy to enjoy the last of the fire by herself.

She took in a deep breath, enjoying the peace. The only sounds around her now were the birds and insects and, a bit farther away, the endless surf crashing on the shore. However, her reverie broke when she spotted a woman heading in her direction from the campsites across the grove. She had a pink amenities kit in her hand, and Lucy guessed that she was headed for the bathhouse.

Lucy's tent was near the entrance to the grove, so the woman would pass right by her. She slipped inside and grabbed her toiletries kit, feeling better about the idea of making the trek when someone else was going. Lucy came out just in time to join the other woman on the path. With the universal smile of welcome between women walking alone at night, they navigated the path in silence and returned the same way.

Lucy turned off the battery-operated lantern and dove into bed. She'd left the twinkle lights on outside, which gave the interior just a little bit of a warm glow. By the time she'd returned from the bathhouse, the temperatures had dropped, and the fog had rolled in thick. She'd waited on her cabin's porch until her walking companion signaled with her flashlight that she was back to her tent.

The light cut through the fog, but the glade around her had become harder to see. The twinkle lights attached to the trees revealed a fine mist of rain falling in the fog. Lucy shivered then and hadn't stopped until she snuggled down in the bed. Not only was there an electric blanket, but the bed's mattress warmer lived up to its promise. She pulled the covers up to just over her nose and tugged her woolen hat down over her ears. It was heavenly to be so snug in the cold night air. Lucy was asleep within minutes.

Lucy wasn't sure what woke her. She'd been dreaming about swimming in the ocean, trying to fight her way out of a rip current. No matter how hard she swam, she just kept getting farther away from shore. It was the kind of dream from which she was happy to wake up.

Then she heard a rustling noise behind her cabin and what sounded like someone walking by. She had noticed a bit of a grassy pathway that ran along behind the tents on her side of the grove and figured it must be for maintenance, as the electrical boxes were behind the cabins.

A knot of fear grew inside her until Lucy remembered that the campground was gated in, with cliffs along one side that dropped to the ocean and someone on duty at the front gate.

Although, there were a few trails bordering the back edge of the campground that meandered through the forest and connected to a state park situated a little farther inland. Afraid to move, she waited for several minutes but didn't hear anything else. She could see her breath in front of her face, testifying to how cold it was outside, so she ignored her bladder and tried to go back to sleep. She'd just begun to doze off when a woman's scream jolted her awake.

Lucy jumped out of bed and slipped her feet into her shoes. Her hoodie and coat were on the chair next to her, so she slid those on before grabbing the lantern from her bedside table. Instead of turning the lantern on, though, she picked up her phone and used the light to find the heavy flashlight in her backpack. It was a present from Mark, who insisted it might come in handy even if she was going to be pampered while glamping. It had several settings that could be useful in different conditions, including fog, but Lucy knew he wanted her to have it as a weapon. She was grateful for his foresight.

More shouts now. People called out from around the grove, some asking what was going on and others yelling for people to be quiet. Above it all, Lucy could hear the frantic cries of a woman. It took her a minute to piece together what the woman was saying—one word over and over. Lucy felt sick as a wave of adrenaline shot through her, propelling her out of her tent when she understood.

Emma.

The hair raised on Lucy's arms as the scream pierced through the fairytale grove again. It was the wounded, desperate cry of a mother for her child.

Turning on her light, Lucy raced across the glade as fast as she dared, hoping against hope that the little girl was okay.

Chapter
Two

The sun was rising over the coastal foothills, illuminating the fog through the branches of the redwood trees and turning everything amber and gold. The ancient forest surrounding her was stunning and beautiful in any light, but the early morning sunshine piercing the fog was unlike anything Lucy had ever seen. The beauty of it only served to highlight the ache in her chest and the knot in her stomach.

The fog hindered the searchers in the dark hours, so they called a halt until daybreak. Captain Andy Harrison had been first on the scene, setting up a command center and calling for search and rescue teams within minutes of arriving. He'd pulled Lucy aside as he waited for everyone to arrive.

"Lucy, are you here by yourself?"

His eyes reminded her of Mark even more than usual in the morning light. The two men shared more than a superficial likeness—they were cut from the same cloth. Both were tall and handsome and held the rank of captain in their professions, it was true. But both men were also honest and kind and bent toward service.

"I am. My grandparents received an invitation to come check this place out before it opens to the public. Everyone here was invited because they have a business in Seaview or, in some cases, because they are new in town. My grandparents weren't interested in glamping, but they thought someone should represent the family."

"Emma's parents told me that she came over to speak with you earlier in the evening. How did she seem to you then?" Andy turned a page in his notebook and looked at Lucy, prepared to take her statement.

"She was happy. She's such a sweet little thing. She came over to thank me for clapping with her. Ed, the owner, and Graciela were here, too, when she came over."

Captain Harrison checked his notes. "That would Graciela Jimenez?" He turned a couple more pages and said, "She's new in town. Received an invitation in the Welcome Wagon package."

"Yes, she's really nice. She shared my fire for dinner, and we had a great time talking and getting to know each other. Her tent is just a few down from mine on the same side."

"What about the owner, Ed Klaas? Did you notice anything off with him at all? Did he seem overly interested in Emma?"

Lucy wrapped her arms around herself and shivered. "No, he was just nice. He'd come over to introduce Gracie to me when Emma ran over. He did thank her and gave her a card for her family to come back and camp again another time for free, but he gave me the same thing. I didn't feel any red flags at all."

"Okay. Thanks, Lucy. Did you hear or see anything else that might be helpful? I can clear you to go home if you want. You're in no way a suspect at this point."

Lucy arched an eyebrow at the police captain. She'd had quite enough of being a suspect after her grandparents disappeared and a string of crimes began, including her own kidnapping.

"I did hear something. It might be nothing, though. I woke and heard footsteps on the path that runs behind the cabins. I figured it was a security guard making rounds, but then the shouting started. I did shine a light back there when we started looking for Emma, but I didn't see anything."

"Okay. Thanks, Lucy. You're free to go. But call me if you think of anything else."

"Andy, I mean, Captain Harrison, would it be all right if I stayed and helped out a little bit? I thought I might call Hattie and ask for some refreshments for the searchers." Lucy gave him her winningest smile. She didn't want to budge until she knew Emma was safe and sound.

Captain Harrison's stomach answered before he could with a rumbling growl. "I think that's a great idea. If I know Hattie, she'll be happy to help."

Lucy and Graciela volunteered to help Kevin—the campfire concierge—make coffee and tea to fill big carafes for the searchers and campers. They set out the pastries and yogurts intended for the camp breakfast until reinforcements from Hattie's café arrived. Several families had planned to cook breakfast over their fire pits, but with Kevin needed for more urgent tasks, most chose to take the to-go option and head home once they were cleared by deputies.

Hattie soon arrived with what must have been the entire breakfast buffet from the café as well as tables and chairs and even several shelters for the food and drinks. She had a small army of teenagers and senior citizens with her, all piling out of several area business vans. They quickly set up a hospitality station near the campground's covered patio, employing Hattie's portable steam tables from the new catering arm of her business. Lucy knew if anyone could pull off a logistical miracle, it would be Hattie. Now she was praying for a miracle of another kind.

Emma's inconsolable parents had been taken to the camp owner's home on the edge of the property—the Klaas residence.

Though they were being looked after by the camp staff and one of the deputies, Lucy knew they must be distraught. A couple of times, the little girl's father had to be restrained from going out to search on his own during the early morning hours. With sheer drop-offs and near-zero visibility, it was too dangerous.

Lucy made containers of food and packed up some hot drinks for the family. They might not feel like eating, but they needed to keep up their strength. She grabbed Kai, one of Hattie's servers, to help her carry everything over to the Klaas house. The deputy was grateful, but neither of the little girl's parents took anything but coffee. Lucy put the containers in the fridge and walked back with Kai. He'd helped Lucy with a fairy garden tea party over the summer during the town's annual Hometown Days celebration.

"Do you think she's okay?" Kai asked in a barely audible voice. Lucy could see the genuine concern on his face. "I mean, the little girl is the same age as my sister. I'd be terrified if Lolly was missing."

Lucy squeezed his arm. "All we can do is hope for the best and help wherever we can. I know Hattie is sending most of the staff back to the café, but if you want to stay, I'll arrange it with her. You can be my assistant for the day, and I don't plan on going anywhere!"

Kai nodded, his golden surfer curls bobbing up and down. "Thanks, Lucy. I'd really like that."

The woman herself met Lucy on her way back to the hospitality shelter with two containers and two drinks. Hattie McMurry, the owner of the Lace Curtain Café, was not only a surrogate grandmother to Lucy, but she was also one of her dearest friends and confidants. The vivacious senior was involved with pretty much everything in the close-knit town of Seaview. Some called her the people's mayor because she was nominally in charge of everything. The current elected mayor was known to defer to Hattie in many cases because people were going to do what she asked.

"Lucy, stop and eat. I know you haven't taken a minute for yourself. Kai, take these over to the table and set it up. I brought you a plate too—and some juice. I thought maybe you could stay here with Lucy. I'll keep you on the clock, and you can just help her with whatever she needs if that's all right with you?"

Kai grinned and took everything from Hattie's hands. "It's like you read my mind, Miss Hattie. Thank you so much. You're the best!"

Hattie called after him, "And don't you forget it! I'm paying you to look after Lucy, but look after yourself too!"

Lucy hugged Hattie. She hadn't seen as much of her as she would like recently. The older woman had been busy expanding her business. First, she'd remodeled the café's back garden and turned it into the most popular spot in town, in even greater demand than the tables in the front garden surrounded by flowers and presided over by an ancient pepper tree that rained tiny white blossoms in the spring. Then she decided to expand further, opening a catering kitchen in the building next door to the café. This also allowed her to expand the café's back garden since the two properties connected. And if that wasn't enough, she'd decided she needed a food truck. It was still being outfitted to her design, but she was very hands-on with the whole process.

"Thanks, Hattie. I appreciate your lending me Kai today. He's having a hard time with all this and will feel better if he's here doing something to help. I guess he's pretty close to his little sister."

"Yes, I thought that might be the case. His mom is on her own raising the two of them, and he babysits when he's not working at the café. Sometimes his sister comes in and sits in the staff dining room and colors while he finishes his shift. She's as good as gold and very sweet." Hattie linked her arm through Lucy's and started walking her over to the table Kai set up. "You eat. I heard that the search and rescue teams on the cliff sides are coming in for a break. I want to make sure everything is ready for them. Then I need to get back to the café. We'll send more provisions as needed, but don't you worry about that. You see what you can do to help Andy find this little girl."

Lucy gave Hattie a peck on the cheek and sat down to eat with Kai. Minutes later, Captain Andy Harrison asked if he could join them. He had a to-go box piled high with pancakes, eggs, bacon, and a large coffee.

"I see Hattie made your breakfast for you." Lucy knew the fit older man loved Hattie's cooking but would never have taken such large portions for himself.

"She did. And she threatened me too. Told me I needed to clean my plate or else!" He gave her a tiny, brief smile. "I just keep going over everything, and I can't understand why this little girl is missing. I decided to let her father join one of the search parties. There's no sign of foul play so far, so that's a mercy, but there's no sign of her. Nothing has been ruled out, but my gut tells me someone picked her up and walked off with her."

"I just don't understand how it could happen." Lucy sighed. "The gates on the long drive up here were locked, and none of the cars that were here last night have moved from the parking lot. The only thing I can think of is the trail that zigzags down the cliff to the beach. But the fog was so dense last night that I can't imagine anyone being bold or foolish enough to risk it. And if someone took her, they'd have to avoid the security patrols too."

"Unfortunately, there were no security patrols last night. I just discovered there was a miscommunication among the staff about who was on duty last night, so no one was making rounds." The police captain pinched the bridge of his nose, squeezing his eyes shut. Lucy could see the pain etched on his face.

"But I heard them. At least, I thought it was the security guard. They were on the maintenance trail that runs behind my cabin. I told you about it. It was shortly before Emma's mom started screaming, maybe just five minutes before."

Andy Harrison had perked up, his eyes blazing with sudden interest. He leaned in toward her. "That's right. I'd forgotten until just now. I assumed you were right. This could be just the break we need. I want you to tell me again. And don't leave anything out, no matter how unimportant it might seem."

Andy called for a deputy to come over. He was one of three new recruits to the Seaview PD, brought on to replace two of the officers who'd recently left the force. One, Officer Mooney, was allowed to retire. He'd been old-school in his approach to policing, and he'd had it in for Lucy from the moment some unusual crimes had taken place in the small community over the summer. In the end, though, he was instrumental in rescuing Lucy, Hattie, Mark, and even his own captain. However, he was past his "sell-by" date, and he had the grace to put in for retirement before it was forced on him. The second officer who left the force, Officer Franklin, was part of an international criminal gang. Thanks to Lucy and her friends, he was now sitting in a jail cell awaiting trial.

The new officer was fresh out of the academy and seemed determined to do everything by the book. Andy asked Officer Jackson to write her statement down and make sure his body camera was turned on to record her answers. The body cameras were new to the Seaview PD, and Lucy knew the reason for them—Officer Mooney had manhandled her and then tried to cover it up.

Lucy recounted everything from the beginning. From waking up, hearing footsteps, and then hearing the heart-rending cries of Emma's mother calling for her.

"Do we have the K-9 team on site yet?" Andy stood and patted Lucy on the back as he addressed his young officer.

"I think they just arrived, sir."

"Well, what are you waiting for, Jackson? Go get them!"

Chapter Three

*I*t was late afternoon, and the mood at the camp was somber. Lucy and Kai were loading things from her tent into her car. He had been very helpful. When a second round of food and drinks were delivered, he took over the entire operation of putting food out and cleaning up after searchers who'd come in for a break. Hattie had trained him well, but it was clear that his work ethic and desire to help were all his own. He'd offered to join the search parties, but only trained search and rescue teams were being allowed to search. Besides, she wouldn't like to tell Hattie if something happened to the young man on her watch.

"Don't leave without giving me your number!" Graciela hurried up the path, pulling a wagon with her belongings. She'd stacked the suitcase and picnic basket precariously, and with every step, it looked as if one or the other of them was bound to fall.

"Oh, I thought you'd left already! I haven't seen you since this morning." Lucy hugged her new friend while Kai took the handle of the wagon and pulled it toward the parking lot. He stopped to shift things around as he waited for the two women to catch up.

Lucy pulled out her phone and tapped in Graciela's number, then sent her a text.

"Got it!" Graciela said. "I was over at the Klaas house most of the day. Emma's mom seemed to find me good company. The poor lady is just going out of her mind, and who can blame her?"

Kai closed Lucy's car and gestured to the parking lot. "Ma'am, can I help you load your stuff?"

Graciela smiled at him. "Such a gentleman! Thank you so much. She held up her key fob and unlocked a car several spaces away.

"Happy to!" he said, smiling back.

Lucy winked at Graciela and whispered, "Oh, I think he's sweet on you."

Graciela laughed. "I could be his mom! Well, much older sister. He's just being nice, I'm sure."

Before Lucy could respond, a shrill whistle cut through the air, followed by two more in rapid succession. What followed was organized pandemonium. Search teams who'd come in to rest and refuel jumped to their feet again and grabbed their gear bags. Police officers swarmed to the command tent for orders. Volunteers serving food and drinks chattered loudly.

Lucy, Kai, and Graciela raced over to the hub of the commotion in time to hear one of the searchers tell a small group of camp staff that three sharp whistles meant either "emergency" or "assemble on me."

Captain Anderson dispatched a small group of searchers with EMT patches on their jackets who carried medical bags. They left on a pair of four-wheelers belonging to the campground and headed along a fire road cut into the forest leading inland. An ambulance crew and two police officers followed in a four-wheel drive truck belonging to the county fire department.

Lucy caught Andy's eye, and he gave her a subtle nod. Relief flooded her body, leaving her weak at the knees. Realizing what this meant, Graciela beamed, and Kai had tears in his eyes. He gave Lucy an impulsive hug, and it was a good thing because she wasn't sure she could remain standing. She continued to lean on the teenager until Graciela caught on and slid a folding chair behind her.

Lucy dropped Kai at home and drove over to the Lace Curtain Café. She'd invited Graciela to join her for dinner, and the newcomer to town had taken her up on it. Hattie was going to want to hear all about it, and Lucy was glad to have someone else help her fill in the details. It had been a stressful hour waiting for the rescue teams to return to the camp. When they did, Lucy didn't see anything except the quick transfer of the little girl, wrapped in foil blankets, onto a gurney that was quickly loaded into the waiting ambulance. Emma's parents waited by the vehicle and climbed in with their daughter as a cheer went up from every corner of the camp.

Graciela and Hattie warmed to each other right away. So much so that Hattie brought out a plate of her own and shared dinner with them. The steaming mashed potatoes and succulent roast beef served *au jus* with roasted carrots hit the spot. The temperature had dropped quite a bit when the sun went down, and nothing could be cozier than a warm, rustic meal. The fresh-from-the-oven yeast rolls didn't hurt either.

Hattie called for one of the servers, who hurried over with a dessert menu.

"Can I tempt you ladies into trying one of our new desserts? They're all recipes from my own mother and grandmother's files, so they're not really new, just new again."

Lucy groaned. "I couldn't eat another bite." She glanced at the menu. "But I would be happy to take a piece of raspberry peach cobbler home for later!" She rubbed her tummy in anticipation.

Graciela looked over the menu next. "Okay, I'll have to make room. I'll have the blackberry pie and ice cream."

"That would be good, but read it again. It's actually blackberry pie ice cream. It's vanilla ice cream mixed with a whole blackberry pie. We serve it in a small dish with a graham cracker crumb pie crust."

"Yes, please!" Graciela licked her lips.

"Okay, you talked me into it. I'll have the same." Lucy sighed. At this rate, she'd need elastic waistband pants in no time. "And I'll take the cobbler to go."

Lucy and Gracie were on the way out when a haggard Captain Andy Harrison held the door for them on his way in. After seeing Gracie off, Lucy turned back into the café.

Scanning the dining room, she headed straight back to Hattie's office just off the kitchen. Her hunch was correct. Hattie had squirreled the officer into the back to personally take care of his order but also to see what information she could get out of him.

Hattie waved Lucy in, and Captain Harrison smiled his welcome. Lucy slipped in and closed the door behind her.

"Lucy, I was just telling Hattie thanks for all the support and supplies she organized for us." He turned back to the older woman. "The county plans to reimburse you for the food costs and use of your equipment. I've already put in the request, so there's no use in telling me no."

"Don't get too big for your britches, Andy Harrison. I remember when you were just a tot, you couldn't get enough of my jammy sammies. I was more than happy to help."

"Well, that's good because I need another favor." Not many people could speak to Police Captain Andy Harrison, who was tall and very fit, the way Hattie could, but he took it with grace from Hattie.

"Just name it." Hattie was tired. Lucy could tell. It had been a long day for everyone. Hattie had been run off her feet at the café because she'd left half her staff to help serve food at the campground. She and the rest of her employees had worked double time to serve the regular customers while continuing to make food and drinks to deliver for the searchers.

"It's for Emma, the little girl who was missing," he said.

Lucy leaned in, very eager to know how her little friend was doing.

"She's physically okay. She was cold and in shock when we found her, but the doctors say she was unharmed." He looked between the women, then continued. "I'm not really supposed to give out information about her condition, but I knew Lucy wouldn't rest otherwise, and well, I think you both can help."

"Anything," Hattie said.

"Absolutely," Lucy echoed.

"She refuses to eat anything. When I saw the food they were serving her, I couldn't blame her! I wondered if you would make her something tempting to eat, Hattie? And Lucy, I'm wondering if you'd come with me to the hospital and bring it to her. She hasn't wanted to talk much yet, but she mentioned you and seeing your tent with all the lights. Her parents agreed. I'm hoping it will help her open up enough to tell us what happened."

Reinvigorated, Hattie jumped up from her desk chair and started shouting orders to the kitchen before she even reached the door.

"I'll be happy to go with you. I need to run home quickly. Do you mind picking me up there and driving? I'm so tired I don't trust myself." The serpentine road to the regional hospital was often foggy, and combined with interrupted sleep the night before, Lucy didn't want to take any chances.

With the plan settled, Lucy hurried out the door. She

needed a two-minute shower and clean clothes. As she eased onto the quaint cobblestone street, her rearview mirror caught the lights of someone pulling out behind her. She sped up, but the vehicle sped up as well, creeping up close to her bumper as if they were impatient for her to get out of the way.

Without signaling, Lucy took a hard right through Artist's Alley. Strings of white lights coiled around the base of each of the trees that lined the street. Several shops had outdoor patios with fire pits or gas warmers where customers enjoyed the autumn evening. Lucy stopped short as a couple with a little girl crossed the street in front of her. Everyone treated the short alley as more of a promenade than a street, so caution was required.

The vehicle following her—a truck with oversized tires—pulled up behind her again. Not quite as close, but too close for her comfort. Spotting an open parking space next to the coffee shop, Lucy claimed it. The hair on her neck rose as the truck moved forward, blocking her from leaving. Lucy took out her cell phone with shaking fingers, ready to call for help.

Before she could unlock her phone, someone knocked on her window. Lucy screamed and banged the side of her fist against the window with one hand and tossed the phone into the air with the other. Eyes wide, she turned her head to see who it was and melted with relief.

"Sam!"

Samuel D. Stevens was the brother Lucy never had. His grandfather, with a near-identical name, had been her family's attorney for decades before retiring and turning the practice over to his grandson. Sam had been instrumental in helping Lucy when she was under suspicion for several related crimes over the summer. The pair had bonded and had an easy relationship. Lucy had trusted Sam with her life and her family secrets. Right now, however, she didn't trust herself not to cheerfully throttle him for scaring her that way.

She rolled down her window to greet her friend, who smiled at her in a goofy manner.

"What's up, Sam?"

"Lucy, have you heard the news? Your grandmother was arrested!" Sam laughed.

Lucy couldn't believe what she was hearing. "What do you mean, arrested? And why is that funny?"

"Well, she's out now. I made sure of that. But it's *why* she was arrested that's so funny. Apparently, she was on her way back from the city, and someone tried to pass her on the right-hand shoulder of the freeway. She wasn't having it and gave chase, and the next thing you know, she's racing this man down the road."

Sam was laughing so hard that he had to stop to breathe.

"Just like a couple of drag racers! Two motorcycle cops came out of nowhere and pulled them over. The drivers were each blaming the other, and—" he panted, "you're never gonna guess who it was!"

Lucy felt as if her head was going to explode. "What in the world? Just tell me. I'm not going to guess!"

Sam needed another minute to compose himself. His face was red, and he held his side while trying to catch his breath. "It was the new padre up at the church, Pastor Delacruz!"

<h2 style="text-align:center">Chapter Four</h2>

Sam decided to accompany Lucy to the hospital, so he parked his truck and hopped into her car. She wouldn't have time to change now and resigned herself to being a bit whiffy for a while longer. If Sam noticed, he was smart enough not to mention it.

Police Captain Andy Harrison's eyebrows raised a notch at seeing Sam exit from Lucy's car. The tall, trim man had recently discovered he was a father to his grown son, Mark, the Coast Guard captain dating Lucy. A tinge of blush crept up on Lucy's cheeks.

"Good evening, Counselor," he said. "Lucy's not being questioned, and she's not a suspect." He winked at Lucy. She'd been a suspect too many times already for crimes she was always cleared of.

"Well," Sam said, "if you must know, considering the gene stock she comes from, I'm just here to keep her out of trouble!"

Lucy elbowed Sam, but Captain Harrison, who had, no doubt, heard about her grandmother's arrest earlier in the day, couldn't suppress a laugh.

"Good luck with that! Call me if you need backup." The police captain gave Sam a mock salute.

"Okay, if you two clowns are ready to go, I'd like to get this over with. I'm exhausted." Lucy walked around to the passenger side of the captain's truck. Both Sam and the older man raced around to open the door for her. Sam opened the back door, and Captain Harrison opened the front. Giving Sam a cheeky look, she hopped into the front seat. She laughed when Sam grumbled about having to sit in the back.

Lucy filled Sam in about everything that had happened. Lucy's voice quavered, and tears threatened to spill over the rims of her eyes as she told him how everyone cheered when the little girl was found. She glanced in the rearview mirror and saw Sam thumbing away his own tears. He was a loveable joker most of the time, but it warmed Lucy's heart to see this softer side of him.

Sam waited in the lounge while Lucy and Captain Harrison took Hattie's to-go boxes to Emma and her family. Even though it was well past visiting hours, the nurse waved them in.

Emma was sitting up in bed, holding a bear and refusing the fruity gel cup her mother was offering. She looked up at Captain Harrison and frowned, but her face lit up when she saw Lucy come around behind him.

Emma's parents, looking weary and wary, welcomed the visitors while Emma reached out a hand for Lucy. She went straight over and ruffled the girl's hair.

"I brought you some super-special dinner, Emma. My friend Miss Hattie made it just for you." Lucy started to open the box on the tray table at the foot of the bed, hoping to get the young girl to eat at least a little bit.

"I ranned to your houth," Emma said.

Everyone's attention turned to the little girl, who had, so far, refused to talk about her ordeal.

Captain Harrison motioned for the girl's parents to stay quiet and let her talk.

"Oh, yes, you ran over after the clapping, right? And the nice man gave you a card for your parents," Lucy replied.

"No, when it was dark, I ranned to your houth." Emma's lisp kept her from pronouncing the word in the usual manner.

"You did?" Lucy held in her surprise and prompted her to continue.

Emma nodded her head. "Yeah, I had to go to the bathroom. I remembered how to get there, tho I went out of the tent. But when I came back, it looked differnt, and I couldn't tell where to go. But I thaw the lighth on your houth. I wath coming there."

"Then what happened?" Lucy's chest squeezed, realizing the little girl was coming to her for help before being lost.

"The man on your porch thaw me. I tried to run away, but he caught me and put a hand over my mouth tho I could barely breathe. He picked me up and ran to the treeth. I tried to kick him, but he jutht kept running. Then I wath crying for my mom, and he put me under a tree with a hole in it and told me, 'Do not move!'" Tears formed in Emma's eyes as she relived what had happened.

Emma's mother pushed past Andy and Lucy and gathered her up in a hug. "You're okay now. You're okay, baby. Mommy's got you."

Captain Harrison wanted to ask more questions, but the doctor came in and made it clear that it was time for everyone to go so Emma could rest. Her father walked them to the door and thanked them for bringing food. Lucy was happy to see that Emma, after wiggling free of her mother's hug, had grabbed one of the containers and dunked chicken fingers into a little cup of ketchup. She was eating them from both fists. Leave it to Hattie to know what even a traumatized child would eat.

Captain Harrison left a deputy stationed outside with instructions to be called if Emma said anything else. Otherwise, he'd stop by again in the morning to see if she could give them any further details about the man or his appearance.

It was a somber ride home. Lucy filled Sam in on what Emma had told them. Both men assured Lucy they would do anything in their power to keep her safe.

She stumbled through the door of the 1880s Victorian house she shared with her grandparents. The harder she tried to be quiet, the louder everything seemed. The boards creaked, the stairs groaned, and even the cat had a loud opinion about her coming home so late. She fed Tor—short for the ridiculous literary name of Victor Admetus Bombalurina from a T.S. Eliot poem on naming cats—and tiptoed to her suite. She stood in the shower for a few minutes, hoping the warm water would be soothing and wash away the stress of the day. But her mind was still troubled as she fell asleep.

Lucy sat across from her grandparents at the small kitchen table. She'd filled them in on her way to Hattie's last night, letting them know the little girl was safe and she was on her way back into town to have dinner with a new friend. Over oatmeal and coffee, she told them about taking food to the little girl and being relieved to see Emma perking up as she was leaving.

She'd left out the detail where Emma described the man being at the door of Lucy's tent-cabin. She didn't want to worry them if she didn't have to. It could be that Emma was mistaken about the man being on her porch, or it could have been a random peeping Tom or someone looking to see what they could steal. Her grandparents were still recovering from a long and terrifying ordeal. They'd been kidnapped, separated, and held captive by an international crime ring looking to discover their secrets and the location of some priceless artifacts the offenders had traced back to her family.

Before she could make up her mind about whether to come clean or not, Captain Harrison appeared at the back door, tapping lightly as he let himself in. His unshaven chin and bloodshot eyes answered Lucy's unspoken question about the rest of his night.

Her grandfather beamed at the younger man, happy for his company. But her grandmother scowled at him.

"I suppose you'll be wanting coffee, Andy Harrison? And let me guess, you haven't taken time to eat yet, either?" Glo stood up and reached for a porcelain cup that said, GOOD MORNING in giant letters. She poured it three-fourths of the way full and asked, "Room for cream?"

"No, thanks. Just black is fine. I can't stay long. I just wanted a quick word."

Glo stiffened and turned her back to the captain. She handed him the steaming drink, but there was anything but hospitality in her stance.

"I don't want to hear it. I've already been lectured." She gestured to her husband, who raised his eyebrows and then winked at Lucy. "I wouldn't have been speeding if it wasn't for that *eejit* trying to run me off the road. I told that officer I was afraid for my life, but he arrested me anyway!" Two red spots appeared on Lucy's grandmother's cheeks.

Lucy stared at her grandmother. She could see the proud older woman was angry and embarrassed, so she stood up and faced the police captain. "Do you really need to rehash it? I'm sure she's good for whatever the fine might be. And maybe you should be looking into the other driver. It sounds like he's the problem!"

Captain Harrison regarded the two women. Anyone could see they shared DNA. Both petite but well-toned, with green eyes that sparked fire when they had strong feelings. Delicate, heart-shaped faces. Lucy's hair was long and strawberry blonde. Her grandmother's hair was snow-white. But both women stood with a defiant fist on one hip.

A smile played at the corner of his mouth before he hid it behind a sip of coffee. "I wanted to have a word with Lucy, Glo. Your, uh, incident yesterday is out of my jurisdiction, but please be careful out there. We wouldn't want anything to happen to you." He gave her a tight smile.

"Oh. Well. Good," her grandmother stammered out. "Carry on."

Lucy, worried about what he might say, started to lead him from the kitchen to the back door. After learning about the trouble she endured in their absence, her grandparents had become somewhat overprotective. Lucy didn't want to give them any more reasons to fret. However, her grandfather stood and followed them out. Very little got past him!

"How's Emma? Is she recovered enough to go home now?" Lucy hoped she could direct the conversation away from any mention of what Emma claimed she saw.

"She's doing great. Eating, playing games on her mom's phone. She does go quiet at times, but from everything she's said and the doctors' conclusions, we're pretty sure she wasn't harmed. Just scared and left alone. Her parents have already found a therapist to meet with her. They seem like genuinely good people. They're blaming themselves, but they really aren't at fault. I think without the fog, Emma would have found her way back to her tent with no problem. Then again, without the fog, she still might have seen the person who carried her off."

Lucy put out her hand and squeezed the captain's arm.

"Thank you for letting me know. I feel so much better. Poor child. I hope she bounces back quickly from this ordeal." She tucked her arm inside his elbow and began to walk toward his truck. "If you hear anything else, feel free to call me. No need to drive all the way over here for minor updates." She gave him her biggest smile, hoping he'd catch on. Her grandfather was following along behind them, just as nosy as anything.

"There's just one more thing. We found shoe prints all the way around your tent. We think someone was waiting there for a while, hiding out. And when it seemed like everyone was asleep, they came to the door of your tent. It wasn't just a random passerby or someone looking for something quick to steal. Emma saw the man there and made a noise, so he grabbed her up and carried her off—to keep her quiet, I presume. That little girl interrupted who knows what. She may have saved your life, Lucy."

*G*lo had retreated to her room, still upset about her brush with the law. Lucy couldn't help but smile. She was sorry her grandmother was unhappy, but the mental picture of her tearing down the highway, drag racing the new pastor, of all people, was hard not to laugh at. At times like these, Lucy really wished Mark had a land-based job so she could just call him and share a laugh.

She pulled out the cash drawer in the bookstore and found it short of bills and change. It was her morning to work at The Cozy Cat Bookstore, and she was looking forward to some peace and quiet in the generally sleepy store. She made a quick call to her grandfather, asking him to pick up change and various bills for her at the bank. He'd gone to Hattie's to have coffee with all the other "seasoned gentlemen" in town. Hattie called them the loafers and looters, but she doted on them, just the same.

On Lucy's desk, well, her grandmother's desk, lay open a large book filled with pictures of Victorian houses, their house plans and blueprints, and a guide to authentic restoration. Lucy hoped that if she found the right color combination, her grandparents would agree to repainting the grand Victorian that was home to not only the bookstore but to her and her family, along with one feisty and overfed cat.

Lucy had fallen in love with a pastel pink, green, and teal color scheme, but her grandparents both vetoed that idea. She'd loved the look of several yellow and white houses, but her grandmother deemed them too cheerful. What she hadn't refused was the paint job the house already had: muted blues with mulberry trim.

Only one thing had been agreed on—the porch ceiling had to be painted "Heavenly Blue." It had always been that color—actually, Haint Blue—based on a superstition that the color kept the haints, or ghosts, away. It was thought that the color would trick them into moving on to the next world instead of haunting the home occupants. Neither Lucy nor her grandmother believed in ghosts, but the tradition was too entertaining to pass up.

Before she had time to settle in with a cup of tea, Tor raced into the room, skidded into her legs, and jumped on the desk. After giving Lucy a glance, he curled up on the book she'd wanted to peruse. When she tried to slide it out from under him, he growled and dug his claws in.

"Fine, you can have it for now. But cats who hog books don't get treats." Tor's eyes narrowed as if considering what Lucy was saying. Then he flicked his tail and turned his face away, dismissing Lucy and her threats.

The bell over the door jangled, and a woman entered. She had a warm smile and kind, blue eyes. She made a beeline for Lucy, bypassing the bookshelves altogether.

"Hi, I'm Sammy Sue Choux." She extended her hand for Lucy to shake, then pulled out a business card.

Glancing at the card, Lucy saw the woman's name followed by the name of a local real estate firm. She'd heard of the company. They specialized in high-end homes and parcels of land if she remembered right.

"Nice to meet you. I'm Lucy. What can I do for you?" Lucy

liked the woman on the spot. There was something honest and forthright about her.

"I'm wondering if you'd have any interest in selling this house. I heard you recently inherited the house and business, and I have a very interested client. They're willing to pay well above market price if you're open to an offer. My client recently moved to the area and is looking to settle here permanently." Sammy Sue pulled a folder from a slim case and offered it to Lucy.

Lucy took the folder as she tried to process what was happening. "I'm flattered by your client's interest, but the house isn't for sale. As a matter of fact, I'm not sure I do own it. My grandparents own the house, which passed to me after they were presumed dead. But it turned out they're not . . ."

Lucy trailed off, unsure whether she should be telling a stranger about the kidnapping and rescue of her grandparents just months before.

Sammy Sue looked disappointed but said, "Well, I thought it was probably a long shot." She looked around the room with an appraising eye. "It's a beautiful house. I wouldn't sell it if I were you either. Keep my card in case you change your mind, and call me any time if you want to discuss it."

Lucy began to hand the folder back to Sammy Sue, who pushed her hand away and said, "Keep it. You might feel differently after you read it."

From the upstairs landing, her grandmother, who'd been eavesdropping the whole time, yelled out, "Oh no, she won't!" before stomping off to her room and slamming the door.

"Sorry about that," Lucy said. "My grandmother has been in a bit of a mood lately."

"No worries. You give me a call if you ever want to find a place of your own." She gave Lucy a sympathetic wink and left the way she'd come.

"Well, what do you think about that, Tor?" Lucy scratched the sweet tuxedo cat's ears and chin. "Should we move out and get a bachelor pad for ourselves?"

Tor just flopped over, his motor purring as he begged for more scritches.

The bell jangled again. Her grandfather came in carrying a to-go cup and several bags. Lucy hurried over to help him, stopping just long enough to give him a kiss on the cheek.

"What did Sammy Sue want?" he asked. "I passed her on my way in, but she didn't have time to stop and talk."

"She came in with an offer for the house." Lucy gestured around the grand Victorian's front rooms, which had been converted into a bookstore before she'd been born. "She has a client who wants to buy it. I told her it wasn't for sale, but she left the offer anyway."

"Hmmm. Let me see it."

"Why? It's not like we can ever sell this house!" Lucy replied. The house was full of secrets that had almost cost them their lives as well as the lives of some of their dear friends. The property had been in the family for more years than California had been a US territory, and the secrets they guarded would have to be kept.

"You got that right!" Lucy's grandmother, Glo, shouted from the top of the stairs. Lucy hadn't heard her return. "Let me see that offer. I don't like the idea one bit, someone poking around our public records and coming here, trying to buy the place."

Lucy hadn't thought about that. Just what sort of information could someone find out about by searching public records? She made a mental note to ask Sam about it the next time she saw the young lawyer. For the time being, she and Sam were still legally the managers of the estate that included her grandparents' home and The Cozy Cat Bookstore. And a charitable trust that had anonymously funded many good works for the people of Seaview.

Sam and his retired grandfather had their hands full working out an inter-generational plan that could move forward without attracting attention from the powers that be. There was an ongoing discussion about whether to revert everything to her grandparents or keep everything Lucy would inherit in her name. Lucy and her grandparents were committed to doing everything on the up-and-up, but some parts of her family's history and how they accumulated their wealth couldn't be exposed. In the meantime, everyone was content to live and work together.

Her grandparents converged on the file before Lucy could open it. As they read over it together, her grandfather's hand started to shake, and her grandmother's face grew red with heat.

"Guys, you're scaring me!" Lucy took the folder from her grandfather's hand and read it for herself. "What in the world? This must be a mistake." The number was shocking, even if it included the business and the property. No one would offer that amount of money unless they had an ulterior motive. From the looks on her grandparents' faces, they were thinking the same thing.

"Call Sammy Sue and have her set up a meeting with this client of hers. I want to know who it is and why they want this house so much." Her grandmother's terse words fell like a heavy weight over the room. A cloud chose that moment to obscure the sun, throwing the room into shadow.

Lucy shivered as a tingle ran up her spine. For the second time that week, she felt a threat looming. Whatever this would-be buyer was up to, it couldn't be good.

Chapter
Six

A swirl of leaves wound around Lucy's feet as she waited for a table at Hattie's café. The Lace Curtain was busier than ever in the run up to the weekend. Locals and tourists alike were excited about the autumn calendar of events in Seaview. There were no less than three festivals in the coming weeks, and almost every business in town participated in some way or another.

Hattie chaired one of the festivals and was on the planning committee for the other two, so her time was limited these days. However, when she spied Lucy, she pulled her out of the line and handed her an apron.

"Lucy, would you mind? I need someone to take drink orders for the garden tables." Hattie gave Lucy a desperate smile and folded her hands in the universal symbol for begging a favor.

Lucy laughed and agreed. She was always happy to lend a hand to Hattie. Hattie had been her mainstay of strength and support when her grandparents were missing and presumed deceased. The older woman had taken great care of Lucy, making sure she was fed and looked after. She'd been a longtime confidant of Lucy's grandparents and was a foster mother to Lucy's boyfriend, Mark.

No two ways about it, Hattie was family, and when family asks for help, you answer the call.

Hattie's renovated back garden was a delightful place to eat. The front garden had long been a popular spot for brunch under the trees or in the middle of king-sized rhododendron and azalea bushes. The back garden had been set up for coziness and privacy, with each table surrounded by greenery, whether a sculpted boxwood hedge or climbing vines blooming on elegant trellises. Each table boasted flowers cut from the gardens and whimsical touches such as red-and-white-spotted ceramic mushrooms for salt and pepper shakers or tiny garden gnomes whose hats served as napkin holders. It was an enchanting place to share a meal, and it was always in demand.

Lucy made her way around the garden, but no one was waiting for drinks. She spied Sam, though, and maneuvered over to his table. He was listening intently to a young woman with caramel-colored hair and mossy green eyes. She was stunning in a cream sweater and matching slim pants. Her oversized sunglasses were pushed up on top of her head in a casual fashion, but her full face of makeup screamed high-maintenance to Lucy. Her pricy bag and shoes confirmed Lucy's suspicion.

"Can I get you a refill?" Lucy asked, waiting for Sam to notice her.

"None for me," the young woman said. Her accent had a fleck of something unusual—just enough lilt to be sweet but not saccharine.

"No, thank you. We're good," Sam replied.

"Are you sure? I'd be happy to bring you a coffee or just top off your ice water." Lucy was a little annoyed. Sam hadn't even bothered to look up.

"Yes, I'm very sure. Just get the check, would you?" Sam still hadn't taken his eyes off his companion, even for a second.

"No charge for you today, sir," Lucy said. "It's on me."

"Wait, what?" That had gotten Sam's attention, and he looked up to see Lucy wink at him.

"Well, gee, thanks!" Sam played along. "I must get Camilla here home, so I appreciate the kind gesture. What's your name again?"

Lucy barked out a laugh. "Knock it off, Sam, and introduce me to your friend."

Sam grinned and said, "Camilla Delacruz, meet Lucy Patterson. Lucy is a client and friend, and Camilla is . . . Well, she's a new friend."

Lucy put her hand out to shake Camilla's, but instead of a greeting, the young woman pressed a twenty into her hand and said, "If you're paying, the least I can do is give you a tip. I know it's a hard life being a server, so please accept this." She followed her words with a tight little smile.

Oh no, she didn't, Lucy thought.

"That's okay. Keep it," Lucy said, putting the bill back on the table. "I'm not really a server. I'm just helping Miss Hattie out. She's a friend."

Sam appeared oblivious to the undercurrent passing between the two women. "Still, it's really nice of you, Luce. Camilla is new in town and doesn't have many friends yet. I'm sure the two of you are going to hit it off. Maybe we can have dinner with you and Mark when he's back in port. It'll be on me."

"Welcome to Seaview," Lucy said. "What brings you to our lovely little town?"

Sam answered for her. "Camilla came with her father. You're never going to believe this, Lucy. Her father is the new pastor at the church." Sam didn't have to elaborate. There was only one church in town with a building and a congregation.

There were other smaller religious groups, she knew, but

none were organized to the point of labeling themselves a church. For as long as anyone could remember, most of the town either attended—or used the services of—the single church that was almost as old as the town itself. It was deemed a historic building, and the view it commanded from its position on a hillside was unmatched.

Most of the bay could be seen from the church windows, as well as the headlands that curved around either side of the town and made a natural shelter. Every sunset turned the interior into a colorful kaleidoscope of reflections from the stained-glass windows. It was a very popular wedding venue for those reasons, and its age and beauty caused it to remain at the heart of the community. No other church had a chance when it came down to it.

"How nice," Lucy said. "I look forward to meeting him."

The woman stood up, causing Sam to push his chair back with unexpected force. Lucy caught it before it tipped backward onto the grass. Sam was so focused on his new friend that he didn't even realize he'd knocked it over.

Camilla gave Lucy another tight smile and put her arm through Sam's.

"I'm sure we'll see you," Camilla said. She paused, then added, "in church."

With that, she led a besotted Sam away. Lucy left the twenty on the table for the crew tips. She'd square up with Hattie for Sam's meal later. In the meantime, though, she realized this was her chance for a table, and she took it,

bussing the glasses and plates and handing them off to a passing busboy who stopped to wipe the tabletop for her.

She'd just settled into Sam's former seat when the hostess approached. It was a teen girl that Lucy didn't recognize, and she wasn't smiling.

"Excuse me, ma'am, you have to wait to be seated. This table belongs to someone else."

Lucy, feeling sheepish, started to apologize. Hattie's had never been so formal or quite so busy before. Before she could get up, though, Graciela came up to the table with a huge smile on her face.

"Never mind," Gracie told the hostess. "This is who I'm meeting for lunch!"

The hostess gave Lucy a suspicious look but nodded and promised to return with a second menu.

"Thanks, Gracie! I snagged this table, but I should have realized there was a line."

"No worries at all. I'm actually thrilled not to have to eat alone. You're kind of making a habit of saving me from eating solo!"

Lucy laughed. "I think we're saving each other!"

Graciela and Lucy were poring over the menu when Hattie herself appeared and pulled up a chair.

"You sweet young ladies mind if I join you? I'm about run off my feet, and Hector is insisting that I take a break and actually eat something!" Hector was Hattie's right-hand man, so to speak, who managed the kitchen and often had to manage Hattie herself.

"Oh, please do! You can tell us what's good today," Gracie said.

Lucy's eyes widened. She hoped Hattie didn't take that as an insult. Thankfully, Hattie's sense of humor was intact, revealed by the wink she gave Lucy.

"Everything is good every day," Lucy said. She nodded and added, "Hattie is not paying me to say that."

Gracie realized her gaffe and made a sheepish face. "Oh, I am sure it is! I just, I mean, well, maybe you could tell us what is *extra* good today? Everything sounds so good that I can't make up my mind!"

"If you both trust me, I'll order for all three of us." Hattie motioned a server over. "Kai, would you bring us one of each of the new sandwiches? But have Hector cut each one into three pieces. Okay? We're going to make our own sampler platter. And bring out a big basket of tater-tots with the sweet and hot sauce, please."

Kai ran to put the special order in, and Hattie leaned forward to speak. "If you ladies like these combos, it'll be on the menu next week. But keep it under wraps, okay? I've noticed the folks from the food truck that rolled into town recently have been stealing ideas from my menu. I needed to come up with something new to keep my customers coming in the door!"

Lucy looked around her. The entire place was packed and buzzing. "I don't understand. It looks like you have all the business you can handle?"

"Well, it's that way now, but I can't afford to sit still while someone systematically erodes my business, you know? Business can turn on a dime, and they seem determined to take mine." The older lady sighed and shook her head.

"I'm sure that must be frustrating," Gracie nodded. "But don't worry. I'll always pick the Lace Curtain. They may steal your ideas, but I doubt they can make it taste the way you do!"

Hattie beamed at Gracie. "You're my new favorite. Sorry, Lucy!"

Lucy laughed. "I'm okay with sharing the top spot. I can't wait to see what you've dreamed up!"

Kai returned with a large tray and a folding table. He opened the table and set the tray down with a dramatic flourish, hamming it up for his boss and her guests. A trio of sandwiches graced each plate, and a platter with a mound of tater-tots threatened to overflow onto the table. There were several silver cups of sauce to go with it.

"*Buon appetito*, ladies!" Kai handed them a stack of napkins from his apron pocket and promised to return in a few minutes with drink refills.

Lucy's stomach gurgled, so she pressed a hand to her midsection. "Excuse me! My stomach knows what's up, though. Hattie, these look delicious!"

Hattie picked up each sandwich in turn, explaining what they were. First up was a toasted, rustic sourdough. She called it the Jacked-Up BLT, explaining that it had a basil pesto sauce, sliced red onions, and pepper jack cheese in addition to the usual ingredients. By all accounts, it was a keeper.

Next, they tried the Veggie Heaven. It had a little bit of everything—grilled mushrooms, caramelized onions, marinated red peppers, and zesty sprouts, to name a few, dressed with simple salt and pepper and garlic sauce that Hattie made fresh every morning.

The last sandwich was served on a hoagie roll stuffed with chicken breast marinated in a sour orange mojo sauce and topped with a cumin-paprika avocado spread. So far, the sandwich was unnamed, but Lucy and Gracie both agreed that it was the best thing they'd ever put in their mouths.

The tater-tots were just standard diner fare, but Hattie's signature sauce was sublime. It was a combination of sweet chili sauce and sambal oelek, a very spicy ground red pepper sauce popular in many Asian dishes. It had a little too much of a kick for Lucy, but Gracie loved it. Hattie typed in a note on her phone to offer a mild version of the sauce along with the hot.

The table grew quiet, then all three women sighed at once. Gracie patted her stomach and grinned at Hattie. "Thank you for letting us be your guinea pigs! If you ever need to try out another dish, call me. I'll come running!"

Lucy laughed. "Hey, that's my job! But you're welcome to join me."

Hattie shooed Kai away when he approached with the check, telling the girls that lunch was on her. "Stay where you are. I'm sending out a dessert to share. I've got to get back to work, but there's no reason you two shouldn't linger and enjoy the garden awhile. It looks like the rush is over for now."

Lucy didn't even think about protesting, even as stuffed as she was. If Hattie was sending out dessert, it'd be rude not to at least try it. Besides, she hated to miss out—whatever it was might never appear again. She noticed Gracie didn't put up a fight either.

"So, I've been meaning to ask, what are your plans? Are you sticking around long-term?" Lucy regarded her new friend. It dawned on her that they'd never gotten around to discussing what Gracie's profession was—or where she was staying, for that matter.

"It's beautiful here, and everyone is so friendly. I've fallen in love with Seaview. I haven't told anyone yet, but I bought a property, and I'm opening a store just off Artist's Alley. I leased a place too. It's just outside of town. There's a retreat center there that has some nice cabins and cottages. They have one a bit farther out on their property that doesn't get much use, so they let me have it for six months. I figure that will give me time to see if I can make a go of things. And if it looks like I can, then I'll be shopping for a house closer to town."

"Wow, that's exciting! What kind of store will it be?" Lucy scratched her head, trying to remember what possible building was vacant near Artist's Alley. The only thing she could think of was McCoy's Trading Post, a relic of a store that had stood empty for many years now. When the previous owners had passed away without heirs, the city ended up with the property. Because it had historical value, though, there were a lot of obstacles for anyone wanting to update it or refit it for another purpose. In the end, it seemed the property was doomed to fall apart for lack of anyone willing to take it on and restore it according to the guidelines.

"Well, I thought I'd try out a combination of things. On one side, I'll have some ladies' fashion and accessories. On the other, I'll have a niche hardware store—everything you need to restore and decorate antique furniture and houses. Since half the houses and buildings in this town are authentic Victorians, I feel there will be a built-in market for that. I know it sounds strange, but I think it's going to work. I've looked around at every shop in town, and I think I can fill a gap here. It will to take a few weeks, though, for the structural work to be finished on the store and for the inventory to arrive. In the meantime, I'm hoping to pick up a side project or two."

"What kind of side project?"

"One that I love, hopefully. I'd like to do some restoration and painting on some of the houses here. My father was a contractor, and I have a lot of experience painting and repairing old houses. I think it's one of the reasons the city was willing to sell the Trading Post to me. I'd love to sand and paint some of the gingerbread trim in town. It's beautiful and gives the town so much charm, but the elements can really take a toll. Some of the prettiest houses have peeling paint and exposed wood that's beginning to rot. It's a total shame, really."

"I think I might have just the thing for you! We've been talking about painting at our house. It's a relic, but it's in good condition. The paint needs updating, especially the porch. Have you driven by it yet?" Lucy had told her about The Cozy Cat Bookstore and a little bit about her family when they'd cooked dinner together at the glamping site.

"Are you serious? I mean, I'd love to come out and look at it and give you a quote, but I'm not desperate or anything. Please don't feel like you have to make up a job for me, Lucy."

"No, really. My grandmother and I have been looking at traditional color schemes for weeks, and we're still not in agreement, but maybe an outside person can convince her that change is good. She has agreed to start the porch ceiling now, though, because it needs it the most."

"Well, then, just tell me when to show up, and I'll be there. I can bring pictures of other work I've done if she'd like. And I have a suggestion: maybe paint that ceiling blue?"

"Yes! We've already agreed on Haint Blue. Only she calls it Heavenly Blue because it sounds better. You've heard of that tradition?" Lucy was pleased to think her new friend was acquainted with the custom.

"Oh yes. I lived for a while in the South. Just about everyone there used to paint their porch ceilings blue. It's a charming superstition, but it also looks good and brightens up a shady veranda without being plain, boring white."

"Well, come anytime. I'm working this afternoon at the shop, but I think my grandparents will be there, and we're all three there tomorrow doing inventory. So, anytime will work." Lucy patted her friend's hand. "Look, here comes Kai." She groaned when she spied what was on the large plate he set on their table. It was a quarter of a pie topped with a tower of whipped cream.

"Here you go, ladies. You're the first to try out the new triple-layer fall pie. The bottom is pumpkin cheesecake, the middle has a maple cinnamon crumble, and the top is a pumpkin-cardamom mousse. The whipped topping is vanilla and maple flavored. Enjoy!" He winked and set down a dessert fork for each of them. "Oh, and this bag is for you to take home, Lucy. Hattie wanted your grandparents to try it too."

Lucy thanked Kai and insisted on tipping him for their meals. She was fond of the teenager and happy to see him enjoying his job. Then she and Gracie made short work of the pie. It was off-the-charts good. Seriously, how did Hattie come up with this stuff?

Chapter
Seven

"I think you should keep the blue." Graciela Jimenez sat across the table from Lucy and her grandmother, Glo.

Lucy had told Gracie her grandmother was stuck in her ways when it came to the house, but Lucy was eager to make some changes. She was beginning to wish she hadn't invited Gracie to meet her grandparents to discuss ideas for the grand Victorian.

"That's what I'm talking about!" Glo shot Lucy a triumphant look. "See, she knows what looks good. Sometimes you have to trust the experts, Lucy."

Gracie grinned. "All you really need to do is update the shade of blue and change out the trim colors. The mulberry color is pretty, but it's really not in style any longer. I think the blue would just pop so much more if you did the accents and trim in dove gray and white. It wouldn't change the character of the house, but it would breathe new life into the exterior."

Lucy was mollified. No doubt Gracie would be a fantastic diplomat, giving everyone something they wanted and pulling together options that everyone could agree on. She looked over the pictures Gracie had loaded on her tablet of houses with similar color schemes and zoomed in on one that had exactly the sort of paint job described. Lucy handed the tablet to her grandmother.

"See? I think this would be beautiful. And it won't go out of style. Just think how amazing your hydrangeas will look next to that!"

Glo pursed her lips—clearly, she knew she'd been handled. She arched an eyebrow at Lucy. "Two against one, is it? Well, I don't hate it. Let's see what your grandad thinks." She looked around and then shouted, "Ulyss! Get in here!"

A rattle and clatter sounded in the kitchen, followed by Lucy's grandfather and their shared cat, Tor, rushing into the room. The startled man and feline managed to tangle themselves up as they burst into the dining room. If it weren't for a convenient, sturdy chair, they'd have ended up in a pile on the floor.

"What's wrong?" Ulysses Patterson, or Ulyss to his wife and friends, grunted as he unfolded himself from over the back of the chair. Picking up Tor, he came around and sat in it. "I thought something happened! Don't scare me like that." He settled the cat in his lap and began stroking Tor's head, causing an immediate loud purr.

Ever since the ordeal the couple had endured over the past year, her grandfather was frailer than Lucy liked and quite a bit more protective than she ever remembered him being. Her grandmother, on the other hand, seemed like a woman re-invented. She was salty, truth be told, and it seemed she'd gone "full Irish," as her grandfather liked to say. By that, he explained, he meant that she was feisty and more strong-willed than ever.

"Oh, don't fuss!" Glo scolded her husband but gave him a wink to show she wasn't serious. "These girls have decided the house needs a facelift, and they want to change the colors. Apparently, the paint we picked out twenty-five years ago is no longer fashionable. Come see what you think of these colors."

Ulyss motioned for Lucy to bring the tablet to him because

Tor had settled in and had his claws hooked into his pants. Her grandfather knew better than to move the cat when he was this comfortable.

"Hmmm. Is this different from what's on it now? Looks about the same to me." He used his fingers to zoom in on the screen. "I like it."

"It's totally different! I swear, Ulyss. It's a totally different shade of blue, and the trim would be gray and white instead of mulberry. Are you fine with this?" She gave him a pointed look.

Lucy knew that her grandmother was hoping he'd come down on the side of just repainting it exactly as it already was. She sat on the arm of his chair and stroked Tor, then kissed her grandfather's cheek. "I think it's really nice! It looks so clean and tidy, and that blue is more natural. It reminds me of the ocean."

Her grandmother gave her a sideways glance. *Uh-oh.* That could mean trouble for Lucy later.

"I do like it. I see what you mean about the shade of blue. I think it's perfect! Let's do it." He put the tablet down and wrapped one arm around Lucy. "It'll be nice," he said to his wife. "A quarter of a century is long enough. It's time for something new."

Before Glo could object further, the sound of voices mixed with the jangling of the door chimes. Sam swept into the room with his new friend, Cami, and their excited chatter caused everyone to focus on the new arrivals.

"Oh good, you're all here!" Sam pulled Cami further into the room. "I was just telling Cami that most of my favorite people live here, and this is the best bookstore ever."

Glo beamed at Sam. She had a soft spot for the young man whose grandfather had been their attorney for many years. He was affectionately known as "young Sam" to her grandparents and their geriatric friends.

"Ulysses and Gloria Patterson, please meet Camilla Delacruz. She just moved to town, and I'm showing her around."

Sam hadn't noticed Lucy sitting at the table off to the side, and she felt invisible for the second time that day. She turned to look at Gracie and realized she was alone. She wondered where her friend had gotten to.

"Call us Glo and Ulyss!" Glo walked over to the younger woman and extended her hand. "Welcome to Seaview. It's a very welcoming town. I'm sure you'll love it as much as we do."

Camilla gave them a demure smile. "Thank you. Please call me Cami. Sam speaks so highly of you all that I couldn't wait to meet you." She looked up at Sam with kitten eyes and a saccharine smile. She was just about batting her lashes, which caused Lucy to roll her eyes and groan.

"Miss Delacruz—sorry—Cami, this our granddaughter, Lucy." Lucy's grandfather gestured over at her.

Lucy caught the quick look of surprise and then annoyance that flashed across the other woman's face before she pasted on a polite smile. "Oh, we've met. You're the waitress from brunch, isn't that right? Do you work here, as well?"

Sam laughed. "Sorry, I didn't see you there, Luce. It was so nice of you to comp our meal at Hattie's." His eyes were full of mischief. She could tell he was in high spirits and enjoying himself as he teased her.

"Oh, no problem. Anything for you, Sam!" Lucy gave same the same wide-eyed, appealing look that Cami had given him just moments before, with just a hint of sarcasm thrown in for good measure. When Cami's right eye twitched and one corner of her mouth turned down, Lucy knew she'd gotten under the woman's skin. It wasn't something she'd normally be proud of, but it was oddly satisfying for some reason.

"I don't work at Hattie's. I was just helping out for a minute. I work here." Lucy didn't feel like elaborating.

"Technically, Lucy owns the bookstore, along with her grandparents," Sam, ever helpful, added. "She inherited it, but then her grandparents turned out to be alive, so we're still untangling everything."

Glo shot Sam a look. Ulyss's neck and ears were starting to redden.

"It's a long story," Lucy said. "We wouldn't want to bore you with the details."

Sam realized his faux pax and, even more, his mistake in discussing his client's personal information. "Oh, yes. Sorry. Like Lucy said, it's a long story, and I shouldn't have brought it up."

"Well, no harm done, Sam. It's bound to come up. The gossips in this town are still wagging their chins about it." Ulyss shifted a now-sleeping Tor from his lap to his shoulder and stood up. "We're pleased to meet you. Come by any time and say hello."

Sensing that the introductions were over—and before things could get uncomfortable—Sam and Cami said their goodbyes. She promised to drop in soon to look around the shop.

They'd just been out the door for a minute when Gracie reappeared by Lucy's side. "There you are! I wondered what happened to you." Lucy's eyes narrowed. "Where were you? I didn't even see you get up from the table."

"It seemed like you guys were busy with family stuff, so I just went to browse the books in the hall, and then I desperately needed to find the ladies' room. What'd I miss?"

"Not much. Just my friend Sam introducing another new person in town. It's so rare anyone close to my age moves here—they're usually moving away—but now we have two at the same time!"

Lucy leaned in and whispered, "You're definitely more my cup of tea, though!"

Gracie barked a laugh. "Well, I'm glad for that because I could use a friend!"

Glo caught Lucy's eye and nodded toward Gracie. "I suppose we should let this one get busy painting the house. I'm sure I'll get used to it. Eventually." Though her words were a little sharp, she winked at Gracie and Lucy and gave them a bright smile.

"You mean I got the job?" Gracie danced up and down on her tiptoes.

"I think you'll do great," Ulyss said. "Send us your estimated timeline, but for supplies, just get what you need at Nuts and Boats and put it on our account. That's our local hardware store. The owner sells used boats in the back parking lot, believe it or not, and he thought the name was a clever play on words. He's the only one who thinks it's funny, though!"

"Thank you so much!" Gracie clapped her hands and hugged Lucy. "I can't wait to get started. Is it okay if I go out the back door and take some pictures of the house from that side?"

"Sure thing, kiddo." Glo seemed more on board now. "The sooner we start, the sooner it'll be done, right? We're closed Monday, so if you want to do the ceiling above the bookstore entrance and that part of the house first, it might be a good time to do it. That way, it won't interfere with customers coming and going."

"It might take me a few days to find some decent help, though," Gracie said. "I want to make sure I hire an experienced, trust-worthy crew."

"Oh, don't worry about that. I'll give you the name of our contractor. He's on retainer. With a house this old, it's a necessity. He'll help you put together a good crew." Ulyss pulled a card from his wallet and handed it to her.

"Then I guess I'll see you Monday!" Gracie squeezed Lucy's arm and skipped through the dining room to the back door.

"I like her, Luce," Glo said. "She has good energy."

Before Lucy could agree, the bookstore door opened again. A lumpy, sallow man shuffled into the foyer, dressed in all black and wearing a hat. She thought he might be Amish, but as he stepped closer, she saw the clerical collar with his suit.

He cleared his throat and spoke with a pleasant tone. "Hello, I'm looking for my daughter. I think her phone might have died, but this is the last location it shows for her."

Lucy couldn't think of any little girls who'd been in the store that morning. She was about to say as much when she clocked her grandmother stiffening beside her. Glo's eyes were wide, and her cheeks crimson.

"YOU!" she hissed.

The apparent minister blinked his eyes rapidly before a look of recognition crossed his face. "What," he growled, "have you done with my daughter?"

Chapter
Eight

*L*ucy sat on a white park bench on the corner of the town square. From her vantage point, she could see the city workers and volunteers setting up for the weekend Art and Wine Faire. It was always a popular event to kick off the autumn season. Only a few trees showed signs of color, but the days were sunny and crisp on the coast.

She bit into the warm apple butter hand pie she'd bought from the DeLiteFull Deli stand. The scent of cinnamon and nutmeg had drawn her straight across the grass, drooling all the way. The warm and gooey filling chased any chill away as she watched the eager artists setting up their brightly colored booths.

She was glad to be out of the bookstore and have a little time to herself. Everything had worked out fine in the end between her grandmother and the new minister, despite it being a little more intense than it needed to be. Sam hadn't introduced Camilla as the minister's daughter, Lucy reflected. Maybe he was hoping they'd get to know her and like her before dropping the bomb on them that her father was the "crazy driver" that landed Glo behind bars.

The minister had tracked his grown daughter's phone to the bookstore—which Lucy found a little weird. Of course, he hadn't known that his road-rage nemesis owned the bookstore.

To de-escalate rising tempers, Lucy had called Sam and told him to bring Cami back to the bookstore pronto.

Once assured that his daughter's phone had died and she wasn't missing, his pleasant demeanor returned, and he introduced himself. He was Humble Delacruz, pronounced "umm-bill," on an exchange mission from Spain. The program allowed ministers to experience different cultures as they accepted positions to supply pulpits the diocese needed to fill.

He apologized for the driving incident, blaming his misunderstanding of the rules of the road in California for his lapse. Glo hadn't been convinced—if the look she gave Lucy was anything to go by—but she'd played nice and apologized too. When he invited them to the service on Sunday, Glo replied that, of course, they'd all be there. After all, it was the church they'd attended all their lives, she'd added. Lucy had worked hard to keep a straight face at her grandmother's territorial remark.

After Sam, Cami, and the minister left, Lucy had said to her grandmother, "Let me know how it goes on Sunday." Mark was returning Saturday afternoon, and they had plans.

Glo had let her know, in no uncertain terms, that the only plans Lucy could possibly have would be to bring Mark and herself to church on Sunday to fill the family pew. Lucy was annoyed. She'd been looking forward to spending the day hiking with Mark, but in the end, she knew Mark would rather not be on her grandmother's bad side. They'd end up squishing together in the pew. That thought had brightened Lucy's outlook—being pressed up against Mark's side with his arm around her didn't sound half bad.

She finished off her hand pie and closed her eyes for a moment, listening to the breeze rustle the leaves on the trees. Feeling upset or worried or annoyed had occupied too much time lately. She took a deep breath in through her nose and held it for a few seconds, then blew it out slowly. It was peaceful in the square, even with all the activity.

In front of the courthouse, vendors assembled rows of art tents and booths and filled them with various creative offerings. The artist's area spanned the entire street on that side of the square. Around the corner, on the library side, many different vineyards and food vendors were arranged across from each other with wide aisles. Lines could get confusing if they were too long, so ample room was needed between each of the tasting rooms and food options. A dining tent on the square close to the library offered seating and shade—or a windbreak—for anyone who needed it.

Lucy's favorite part of the Art and Wine Faire was the separate row of jewelry makers positioned at an angle on the street between the courthouse and library. A blockade at the far end of the road created a nice "Boulevard of Bling," as announced by a waving banner. She looked forward to checking out the designs available and hoped to pick up a few strands of beads to make something.

The sun was a little lower in the sky by the time Lucy was ready to move from her perch. Before long, the live music would start, and the mayor would welcome everyone to the festival. She liked that the activities began on Friday afternoon. It allowed the locals to shop with smaller crowds, for one thing, and it always turned into a bit of a town party by the time the sun went down.

She stretched her legs and hips out from sitting too long and tossed the hand pie wrapper. All she wanted to do now was cut loose and have a little fun. The band started to play, so Lucy joined the crowd heading toward the stage.

It was a Bangles tribute band, which suited Lucy just fine. She was ready to walk like an Egyptian and soon had a flock of little girls dancing with her. She knew most from the bookstore or other town events and enjoyed hanging out with them. Their parents never seemed to mind—mostly likely happy to have a responsible adult entertaining their kids for a few minutes. The next time the chorus hit, and Lucy put her hand out behind her to do the iconic dance, someone grabbed her hand and squeezed it hard.

She whirled around to see who it was. "Emma!" She squeezed Lucy's hand even harder. Her whole little body was shaking—her neck stiff with terror. Lucy bent down to her level.

"Emma! What's wrong, sweetheart?" Lucy pulled her into a hug, afraid for the little girl. The child's parents parted the crowd to get to them, which was a relief. Was Emma reliving what had happened to her? Did seeing Lucy trigger bad memories?

Emma was saying something over and over, but Lucy couldn't make it out. She put her ear directly in front of Emma's mouth, not letting go of her for a second. "He'th here. I thaw him. He'th here."

Lucy looked around, her eyes searching the crowd, but she didn't know what to look for. "Where is he, Emma?"

The girl refused to raise her eyes and look. She clung to Lucy. The song ended as Emma's mother scooped her into her arms. The dam burst, and Emma's sobs covered her mother in tears.

Her father asked what had happened. Lucy told them what Emma had said, and a look of fear and disbelief crossed their faces. The band started a new song, "Manic Monday," while Emma's parents both held on to her, sandwiching her between them.

"We should call for help," Lucy said.

"No! We need to get her out of here. Our car is right over there." He pointed to a row of parking spaces on the other side of the square. "She's been having nightmares. Maybe seeing you caused her to remember the ordeal and made her think she saw him. We just need to get her home."

Emma piped up, "I did thee him! I did! He thaw me too!"

Emma's dad lifted her up and away from her mother. "Let's go. We can call from the car."

"I see Captain Harrison over by the stage, I'll tell him what Emma said, and you guys can go ahead and get to safety and then call it in." Lucy patted Emma's back. "It's going to be okay, sweetheart. We're going to find that guy, and he'll never bother you again."

Lucy could only hope she was right. If the man realized that Emma had recognized him, it could spell trouble for the little girl. Then Lucy remembered that the man seemed to be watching her glamping tent and a shiver went down her spine. And just like that, Lucy wasn't so happy to have time to herself.

Lucy reached down and readjusted the strap on her sandal. It had been some time since she'd worn the pretty but impractical shoes, and she already looked forward to taking them off.

Mark had been delayed onboard his ship, a Coast Guard cutter he captained. Lucy had been disappointed—it seemed his job was taking him away from her more often and for longer stretches of time. However, she knew it was just part of dating someone in the U.S. Armed Forces, so she was determined to make the most of their time. Thankfully, Mark was happy to accompany her to church with her grandparents.

The four of them sat thigh to thigh in the small pew. Glo had insisted they arrive early so they could occupy the pew donated by Ulyss's grandfather. It was a point of pride to sit in the Patterson pew if you were a Patterson. A small brass plaque on the wall marked the donation in memory of his beloved mother, Ardelia Patterson. Not that they attended all the time, but when they did go, it seemed disloyal to sit anywhere else.

Lucy tried to pay attention to the sermon, but something about the minister's voice caused her to zone out. Being mesmerized by the stained-glass windows didn't help either.

As a child, she'd loved the stained-glass windows and imagined they were secret doors that led to other, more beautiful worlds. The church faced the water, and high above the entry was her favorite window of all. The round window, framed with rich mahogany wood, displayed a coastal scene of intricate patterns and beautiful colors. However, it was the only one remaining that was original to the building. The others had been destroyed by a storm and replaced in a later era. They were beautiful but couldn't match the artistry and craftsmanship of the earlier ones. This one even had a name: The Porthole to Heaven.

Lucy felt a subtle elbow digging into her ribs and glanced at her grandmother. She was giving Lucy the "pay attention" look. Lucy knew it by heart from many times before while sitting in the very same seat. She gave her grandmother a wink and then made a point of schooling her face to look at the minister with rapt attention. In her peripheral vision, she saw Glo roll her eyes. Lucy held in a chuckle. If she'd still been a kid, or even a teen, an earful about her attitude would have followed the service.

She glanced at Mark, but he, too, was giving a look. *Fine, I'll be good.* She gave him a sweet, innocent smile. *For now.* He gave another look that seemed to say he wasn't buying her act. He started to stretch and put an arm behind Lucy on the back of the pew but aborted halfway.

Lucy and Mark both sat straighter in their seats and kept their eyes focused ahead. Neither of them even twitched until it was time to stand and sing the closing hymn. They didn't dare— Hattie was sitting behind them and had poked them both in the back with a whispered threat of not saving them any chocolate cobbler if they didn't behave. The promise of chocolate cobbler was enough to turn even the most mischievous into choirboys and saints!

As soon as church was over and everyone exchanged greetings, Lucy and Mark decided to visit the bathrooms before heading out. As always, there was a longer line for the women's than the men's. Mark wasn't waiting when she came out, so she went back down the hall to check the sanctuary. But he wasn't there either. No one was. The church had pretty much cleared out already.

She retraced her steps, thinking perhaps Mark was still in the men's restroom, but no one answered when she cracked the door and called. She went farther down the hall to see if Mark had gone to check out more of the building.

Then a woman laughed. "Oh, my hero, you saved me!"

That voice. *Where have I heard it before?*

Lucy pushed open the door to the minister's study. There stood Cami in Mark's arms, kissing him directly on the mouth.

Lucy was quiet on the way to the dock. She couldn't get the image of that woman making a play for Mark out of her head. Mark had pushed Cami away and stepped back. His back was to Lucy, but Cami saw her standing in the doorway, and Lucy could swear she smirked. Instead of being deterred, the woman reached for him again, saying she needed to thank him properly.

Mark had evaded her grasp and told her it wasn't necessary. He'd turned and seen Lucy then, and his face changed from embarrassed to angry. He stalked toward her and took her arm before turning around to address the minister's daughter. "You really should be more careful, Miss."

He'd pivoted and pulled Lucy from the church before explaining that the strange woman had asked him for help in her father's study to reach something on a shelf. Instead of pointing it out to him, she asked him to hold the ladder and then made a show of falling, forcing Mark to catch her.

Lucy had laughed at first. Who could blame her? Mark was an incredibly good-looking man. He was tall and very fit and had eyes the color of green sea glass. But then she remembered that Camilla had sat a few rows behind them—there was no way she didn't know Mark and Lucy were together. It was all a ploy. Whether it was meant to entice Mark or annoy her, she wasn't sure.

But the more she thought about it, the angrier she became. She didn't blame Mark—she trusted him—but it did seem that Cami was intent on antagonizing her from the beginning. It disturbed her that Cami seemed to have her hooks in Sam and was flirting with Mark at the same time. Lucy often joked with Sam that he was the little brother she never wanted, but she cared a great deal about his happiness and didn't want to see him hurt.

When they pulled up to the dock, she decided to put the bad feelings behind her and enjoy the day. Mark had arranged to borrow a boat from a friend and planned a picnic near a small island not far offshore. She had a change of clothes and shoes in a backpack stowed in Mark's truck, which was a good thing because church sandals stood no chance of surviving the rocky shore.

The boat was much nicer than Lucy expected, gleaming white with freshly polished chrome and pristine teak decking. She kicked her shoes on the dock and walked barefoot up the ramp after Mark. The *Endless Summer* was too big to be called a mere boat but just shy of being a yacht. It came equipped with deck chairs and a sunning pad, and inside consisted of a lounging area, a galley, and a spacious head. Mark pointed out a compact spiral staircase that led down, saying the captain's quarters were below if she wanted to get changed.

The bedroom was small but well-appointed. She blushed after noticing a decorative life preserver on the wall that read "S.S. The Love Boat." It was cute, but the implications didn't bear thinking about. She and Mark had agreed to take things slow, and considering how often Mark was away with the Coast Guard, slow meant very slow. She put on a pair of capri-length jeans, a white T-shirt, and a faded blue sweater she'd stolen from her grandfather. It was the perfect weight for a sunny but breezy day on the water.

When she returned upstairs to the bridge, Mark had the engine idling and ready to go. Lucy helped him drag in the ropes and secure them on deck as they drifted away from the dock. Mark expertly turned out of the marina and headed out into the bay, setting course for Refuge Island. The island was only about a mile long, but it had a deep bay on one side with a gently sloping beach backed by uncut forest. It was a popular place for sightseers and campers, but as soon as the off-season began, it was deserted.

Lucy took two bottles of water from the cooler Mark had rolled on board and opened them both, handing one to him. She'd caught him up via phone late the night before concerning everything from the past week. To say that he hadn't been happy was an understatement. Neither of them said much on the way to church, and they'd only spoken about necessary things after. The silence was growing a bit awkward.

Lucy walked around behind the panel where Mark stood to navigate and put her arms around his waist. He smiled and drew her around the side, keeping one arm wrapped around her middle.

"Luce . . ."

Lucy sighed. Everything felt right with the world when she was next to Mark.

"Don't tell me. I know. You want me to stay safe and not go anywhere alone and keep my phone on and in my hand and keep my head on a swivel so I can see trouble coming. You want me to lock myself in my room until they catch whoever it was that kidnapped Emma and was staring into my tent. Am I close?" She winked at him.

He bit back a grin and said, "No, I was gonna ask you to hand me a sandwich."

They dropped anchor just inside the natural harbor. Many ships had weathered strong Pacific storms in the same place, but today the sky was as blue as a sapphire, and the water washed ashore in smooth and hypnotic ripples. They ate lunch on deck, basking in the sunshine. Lucy almost allowed herself to be lulled to sleep, but she didn't want to miss a minute of being with Mark.

Mark had made the entire picnic himself. Simple tuna salad, grapes, tangerines, and salty kettle-cooked chips had never tasted so good.

She didn't want the day to end.

"What do you think, Lucy? Should I retire and buy a boat like this? We could spend our days sailing all over the world, exploring, sleeping under the stars, swimming, and fishing, and going wherever the wind takes us . . ."

Mark's face was dreamy as he gazed at the open ocean beyond the island, but a small knot began to form in Lucy's stomach. In her heart of hearts, she knew she was tied to the land, and she was feared she was going to lose Mark to the sea. She had thought he wanted to retire and settle down on land with her, but now she wasn't so sure.

"It sounds like an adventure," she said.

Mark didn't notice her hesitation. "It sure would! The adventure of a lifetime *for* a lifetime!" He kissed Lucy on the forehead and made his way down a small stairway to the stern deck.

Lucy could picture herself spending a lifetime with Mark, but not as his first mate. An image of herself dressed as Gilligan, hat and all, flashed through her mind. *Yeah, not a good look.* Now wasn't the time to discuss it, though, because Mark was pulling down a platform attached to the back of the boat.

An inflatable dinghy rested on it, and Mark went inside the stowage compartment to pull out a hose and the anchor. He made quick work of filling and prepping the boat and attaching the motor. He added in personal floatation devices and a pair or oars as safety precautions. After checking that the anchor was set and telling Lucy all about the excellent ground tackle on the boat's anchor—which went right over her head—he was ready to take them into the cove.

Lucy had to admit, it was kind of exciting to step into the small boat and go ashore. She trailed her hand in the water, letting the chilly Pacific numb her fingers. The water in the cove was calm, and there was no breeze at all on the protected leeward side of the island except what riding in the small craft generated. The sun turned the shallow water a beautiful shade of turquoise that she tried her best to capture on her cell phone. Such a beautiful day deserved a spot in her photo albums.

Mark ran the dinghy ashore, hopped out, and then lifted Lucy out of the boat. She was grateful for the assist and happy not to have wet feet. Smooth stones, ground down over time with the tides, littered the shore. Just beyond them were gravel beds of finer rocks and shells. As they walked, Lucy scanned the ground for any rocks that stood out.

It only took seconds to spy a purplish agate. She grabbed it and held it up to the sky, enjoying the translucent bands of color in the stone. Next to her, Mark picked up a carnelian agate and gave it to her. She kissed his cheek in thanks for the golden-hued specimen. They spent half an hour combing the shore, Mark storing the agates for her in his pockets. By mutual consent, they decided they had enough and headed further up the beach.

Then Lucy spotted a bright red stone, almost the color of cherry candy, sitting all by itself. She ran to scoop it up and crowed. It was the best one yet, maybe the best agate she'd ever seen. Mark made appropriate noises over her prize, which Lucy refused to hand over just in case he developed a hole in his pocket. She'd found a treasure, a keepsake to remember the day.

The sun was starting to sink behind the top of the island, throwing the trees into shade. With it, the temperature began to fall, so they decided to take just a short hike along one of the paths leading into the tall trees. They followed a trail that led uphill and gave them occasional breaks in the trees with a sightline to the boat. Each time they broke through, Lucy felt relieved to see it was still there.

Their vantage point on a small bluff provided a view across the water to the mainland.

"It seems so far away," Lucy said. She gestured across the water.

"Yes. Imagine being stuck on this island, seeing shore, and not being able to get there." Mark was referring to the legends that the island had played host to some shipwrecked crew a long time ago, men who had spent months trying to survive before they were discovered.

She shivered, remembering the legend said several had died here waiting for rescue.

Mark put an arm around her, warming her up. She snuggled into his side, appreciating his warmth and his thoughtfulness. He pulled her around until they were face to face as he held her in both arms. His eyes said he wanted to say something, but then he seemed to change his mind and kissed her instead.

The kiss left her breathless, and she hadn't wanted it to end. But an alarm sounded on Mark's phone.

He shut off the alarm but groaned as he looked at the screen.

"Come on, Lucy, we have to hurry back. That was the anchor drift alarm. We need to get back to the boat before she takes off without us!"

Thankfully, the dinghy got them back to the boat in good time, and Mark was able to secure the line and pull up the anchor before it tangled. They deflated the dinghy and stowed it away before Mark pointed the vessel's nose toward the windward side of the island. They took a quick ride around the other side before setting course for home. Once they were out away from the shadow of the island, Lucy lounged on the deck, enjoying the sea air and sunshine for as long as she could. Maybe living on a boat wasn't such a terrible idea? However, as they drew closer to shore, she felt more than ready to disembark.

When Mark curved the boat around to approach the marina, a glorious portrait captivated Lucy's attention. The sun was low in the sky, shining into the round stained-glass window of the church. It cast such brilliant illumination into the building that all the side windows below glowed with light too. It made a stunning image, nestled into a row of dark houses on each side. Something stirred deep inside Lucy's memory, but she couldn't quite put a finger on it. She pulled out her phone and snapped a picture. This one she'd post on her social media accounts.

They capped the evening off with dessert at Hattie's before Mark drove her home and kissed her on the cheek to say good night. That was all he could do, given that Lucy's grandparents were sitting on the porch, and her grandmother was giving him a fierce glare. Lucy giggled. You'd think she was still a teenager who stayed out past curfew!

She kissed her grandparents goodnight before heading inside to have a long hot shower. She placed the gorgeous agate on her dresser, admiring once again the crimson glow.

"What a perfect day," she said to Tor, who yawned in reply. Thinking of Cami's play for Mark in the church study, she added, "Well, almost perfect!"

Chapter
Ten

Lucy woke up to the sound of voices downstairs. She couldn't make out what they were saying, but she could tell that someone was upset and raising their volume. Wiping the sleep from her eyes, she reached for her phone. A quarter past seven. She groaned and pulled a pillow over her head, but it did no good. She was awake now, for better or for worse.

She spent ten minutes getting ready for the day—hair in a bun, jeans, tee, and a hoodie—before running down the stairs two at a time. Tor followed and then darted ahead of her toward the dining room. She smelled bacon. Surely nothing could be too wrong if there was bacon, right?

She rounded the corner just in time to see her grandmother throw a cinnamon bun at Dr. Larry Wilson's head with full fury. Thankfully, the older gentleman's reflexes were still pretty quick, so he caught it instead of having a face full of cream cheese frosting. He set it down on the plate in front of him and shook out his napkin with his clean hand.

"Grandma!" Lucy was shocked. Her grandmother had always been a little feisty, but she was never unladylike. Until recently, that is. Lucy shook her head. "I can't believe what I'm seeing! Why did you chuck a pastry at Dr. Wilson's head?"

Her grandmother was obviously fit to be tied. She didn't answer Lucy but turned and stalked into the kitchen.

Lucy took stock of the table and the people sitting around it. Her grandfather sat at one end, looking as if he wished he were anywhere else. Dr. Wilson sat on his right. Glo had vacated the seat to his left, and down from there sat Hattie, who sipped her coffee and avoided eye contact with Lucy. It appeared they were about finished with a feast. Platters with the remains of bacon and scrambled eggs and biscuits sat in the center of the table, along with a bowl of sausage gravy, cut fruit, and a dozen different pastries.

"Does somebody want to tell me what's going on here?" Lucy was a bit peeved. Being awakened too early often had that effect, but missing out on a stellar breakfast because no one had invited her just felt like adding insult to injury.

No one answered Lucy. In fact, everyone seemed to busy themselves with eating or drinking or pushing food around on their plate. Hattie flashed Lucy a sympathetic smile but said nothing. Finally, her grandfather put his knife and fork on his plate and pushed back from the table.

"Lucy, there's plenty left for you. You can microwave it if you want something hot. We didn't want to wake you." He shifted from foot to foot, which Lucy knew meant he was not happy about something but trying to hide it from her. "Come and sit down."

Lucy sat next to Dr. Wilson and leaned in to speak. "I'm so sorry. I apologize for my grandmother's behavior," she said. "I don't know what's gotten into her."

Even though she'd spoken softly, a loud bang came from the kitchen that sounded like a pan whacking the stove.

"I'd better go . . ." Her grandfather shuffled off to the kitchen where his long-time bride was venting her frustrations.

Dr. Wilson, unperturbed, finished wiping off his hand and smiled at Lucy.

"What can I get you?" He motioned to the tray of pastries.

Lucy's stomach betrayed her by growling, so she nodded yes to the tray of sweets and took a large cinnamon roll with the tongs. She eyed the platter and added a banana nut muffin to her plate as well. While she did that, Hattie poured her a cup of coffee and pushed the sugar and cream her way.

"Would somebody please tell me what happened? Why is everyone here so early? And why is my grandmother throwing pastries at you?" She raised her eyebrows at Dr. Wilson in what she hoped was an authoritative manner.

"Eat first." He patted her arm. "Plenty of time to discuss matters, but you should try to eat something."

"Fine," Lucy ground out. She bit the muffin. Mmm. Honey's Bakery. She'd know that flavor anywhere. She took a sip of coffee and had another bite. Before she could ask again, Hattie passed the bacon, followed by the eggs, biscuits, and gravy. She dutifully took a portion of each.

She ate half the stick of bacon and waved the other half in the air, pointing it at each of her "well-seasoned" friends in turn. "Okay, I'm eating. Now talk!"

Hattie sighed. "We had a meeting."

"I can see that, Hattie. About what?" Lucy crammed the second half of the bacon into her mouth and waited for an answer.

"Well, it was about you." Hattie looked at Dr. Wilson, but he just waved for her to go on.

"Me? What did I do?"

"No, you didn't do anything. It's just, well, you have a lot going on. New friends, a new boyfriend, the changes you want to make to the house and garden . . ." She trailed off.

"And?" Lucy was growing impatient.

Dr. Wilson cleared his throat. "Well, as you know, there are certain things that need to be kept, you know, quiet. And the general feeling is that maybe you should focus on enjoying your life and not worrying so much about the bookstore or the foundation, that sort of thing." He looked toward the kitchen, but no reprieve was coming. "You know that we're part of your grandparents' circle of, er, friends and trustees, and there's an idea being put forward that perhaps you should, um, move out of the house for the time being." His face reddened—as he knew the words would be hurtful to Lucy.

"So, I'm being cut out. Is that it?" Lucy was furious. "Where's Sam? Why isn't he here?"

Hattie reached across the table to pat Lucy's hand. "No, it's not like that, Lucy. Besides, some of us don't agree. We couldn't come to any sort of consensus at all, and things got a little bit heated. I'm sorry we woke you up."

Lucy couldn't swallow the coffee she'd tried to gulp down to hide her tears. Her throat had grown painfully tight and remained so, even after she finally choked it down. "I won't stay where I'm not wanted." She rose to her feet, hitting the table and causing her coffee cup to slosh over into the saucer. "Hattie, do you still have a room available? I'm going to need a place to live."

Her grandfather hurried back into the room.

"Hang on there, Lucy. You're taking this all wrong. I don't want you to go. We're just . . . worried. Worried that if you stay here, if you stay too close to things, you could be hurt. You should be out having fun, going out with Mark, enjoying your-self, not worrying about . . ." He waved his hand toward the wall of the Victorian, where a hidden panel contained a secret staircase. "You shouldn't have to take on this burden too soon. And it is too soon. Ideally, you'd be your parents' age before you even found out about, well, what lies beneath." Her grandfather used their favorite code word for the hidden rooms and tunnels beneath the home—some man-made and some carved out by nature—that contained their family's long-standing secret.

Lucy's hurt was too big for her to hear the pleading tone in her grandfather's voice. She turned to Hattie and said, "I'm going to need a job too."

"Lucy, sweetheart, my door is always open to you, but maybe let's take a minute to think about this." Hattie's eyes were rimmed with tears. "I think the whole kidnapping thing has really thrown everyone for a loop. Your grandmother just doesn't want anything to happen to you. Especially after what happened to her."

Lucy's face softened a little. She wasn't unsympathetic to what her grandmother had endured this past year, or her grandfather either, for that matter. But ever since they'd returned, she felt like an outsider. After the initial debriefing, they had pretty much clammed up and not wanted to talk about their experiences or the centuries-old treasures they were custodians of. At first, she'd thought they just needed time to process and get back to normal life, but now it seemed that they didn't want to talk to her about it at all. She felt frozen out since they'd had a breakfast meeting with all their friends to discuss it.

The other problem was that Lucy had nowhere else to go. She'd moved to Seaview and settled in, planning to make a life for herself in the beautiful Victorian house and running The Cozy Cat Bookstore. It was what she'd always wanted to do.

"I'm not a child," Lucy said to no one in particular. "I can take care of myself, and I've proven I can handle things when it comes to the family secret. Surely I've earned everyone's trust."

Glo came back into the dining room from the kitchen. "It's not that simple, Lucy. It might have been fine to leave things the way they are, but now the secret seems to be out, which spells trouble for all of us. One person has already died because of it. We can't let that happen again."

She referred to Fuchsia Butterfield. The older lady had first accosted and later helped Lucy when Glo and Ulyss's kidnappers tried to get Lucy out of the way so they could take whatever they found for themselves. In the end, Fuchsia paid with her life.

Lucy closed her eyes. Yes, her grandparents were worried about her. But they didn't seem to understand that she felt responsible for keeping them safe every bit as much as they did her. This was her home too. She was determined to be more involved, not less. There was still so much she didn't know but was determined to find out. There were four rooms in the basement that she'd never been allowed to enter. She felt sure that her grandparents hadn't told her everything about the house and her family or their multi-generational caretaking of what was hidden below.

She knew some of the history, but there were large gaps in her knowledge—she was sure of it. The people seated around this table were the only ones who could tell her what she wanted to know.

She opened her eyes and looked at each of them in turn. Ulyss squirmed under her gaze, but Glo stared back. The defiance and determination on her face caused Lucy to narrow her eyes.

"I'll think about it," Lucy said. "But first, I want to see the compass rooms, and I want to know the whole story, not just the bits you think I can handle, Grandma. And I want to know now." She lifted her chin and titled her head to show she meant business.

"I hope I'm not interrupting?" A new voice spoke from the opposite end of the dining room. Gracie stood there in painter's overalls with her hair pulled through the back of a cap into a thick ponytail. She held a paintbrush in one hand and a bucket in the other. "The door was open, so I just let myself in. I wanted to let you know that we're getting ready to tape the windows and start work on the front porch if that's okay?"

"Of course, it is. Go right ahead," Ulyss answered. "We'll be out to check in with you in a little while. Why don't you take the pastries out with you?"

Gracie grinned. "I'm sure the guys would love that!" She scooped up the plate, managing to give Lucy a quizzical look on the side. "Lucy, could you help me? I'm not sure I can carry everything without dropping something."

Lucy rose, took the plate from her, grabbed a stack of napkins from the table, and followed Gracie out. The worry knot in her stomach was back. Exactly how much of that conversation had Gracie heard? And why hadn't the bells over the door jangled to warn them someone had come inside? It seemed all Lucy's questions would have to wait.

*G*racie was a complete professional. Even Glo had nothing to complain about when it came to the quality and speed of the work. She had a fantastic crew—a combination of local painters and craftsmen found through Ulyss's contacts and a couple of other specialists she'd hired to ensure the historic integrity of the home was preserved. She did many of the artistic trims herself, not trusting anyone else to paint the gingerbread attachments that gave the house such special character.

Lucy kept Gracie company a few times after the crew had gone home for the night. She would often start work on trim when it was quieter and there were fewer people around. It took patience and focus, as Lucy learned when she offered to help. When the air became chilly or the light started to dim, the two often had a quick bite together before Gracie went back to town to work on her own store renovation.

"Are you sure you're not overdoing it?" Lucy asked. They'd just spent several hours painting railings a beautiful dove white, and now Gracie planned to spend the rest of the evening sanding floors at the former McCoy's Trading Post.

"I probably am overdoing it, but the money I'm earning for this job is helping to pay for the work the store needs before we open. It's cost a bit more than anticipated, so I'm glad to have the chance to overdo it."

Lucy felt bad for her friend, who was doing most of the work alone at the store. "Well, I'm going with you. I don't really love the idea of you being there alone at night, especially since you're already worn out when you get there."

"You don't have to do that!" Gracie was adamant. "I can manage, Lucy. I promise. I'm used to working, and I enjoy the work. I'm excited to see the progress each night. We'll be opening before you know it, and your house will be finished in a couple of weeks. I can rest then."

Lucy laughed. "Yes, because opening a brand-new business and doing all the work and advertising yourself is a really good way to get extra rest." She took the paintbrush from Gracie's hand and dropped it in a bucket of water for rinsing. "I'm coming with you. Let me just tell my grandparents not to plan on me for dinner. Besides, it'll be fun to see what you're doing there. The whole town is buzzing because you have the windows and doors papered over and they can't see inside."

"Okay, fine. I wouldn't have this job if it weren't for you, so I guess you can have a sneak peek. But I will put you to work!"

Lucy pulled out her phone. "I guess I'd better order us some dinner then! We finally got Dinners on Demand in town, so our food will be there by the time we are!"

Lucy hadn't been inside the McCoy's building since early in the summer when she had followed Mark inside. He'd been working on bringing down a smuggling ring as part of an interagency task force, but Lucy hadn't known that. By the time Lucy made it to the building, someone on a motorcycle had taken off from the back of the store, and inside she'd found Mark injured and barely conscious on the floor.

She shivered at the memory but forgot about it when seeing the inside of the store. Lucy admired each detail. The freshly painted walls. The glass displays that came with the store—now gleaming and ready for new merchandise. The built-in shelves along one wall all polished like new. The clean floor—even though the finish was worn and uneven.

The two main rooms had a wide opening between them. On the far wall, a deep fireplace featured a large iron bracket called a crane. The hinge on one side enabled a cook to hang a pot over the fire. On the side of that room where the original bedroom was previously located, a former tenant had added a small office and bathroom nestled between deep, built-in shelves. No matter what the merchandise, the store was going to be beautiful.

"It looks so good in here! I can't believe it's the same place." Lucy ran her fingers along the polished oak doorframe. "Really, you've done wonders. I can't wait to see this place with everything in it!"

Gracie beamed at her. "I'm so glad you think so. I have butterflies every time I think about actually opening the store." She motioned for Lucy to follow her into the back room, where a small folding table and chairs were tucked into a corner. "Let's eat. I'm starving. But after that, don't feel as if you have to stay. I only have one sander, so I'm not sure what you can really do."

Lucy pulled the Thai food from the bag that had, indeed, been waiting for them by the door. Seaview was lucky to have such a good Thai place in a small town, and Lucy felt fortunate to have someone to share her favorites with. The pumpkin red curry served over fragrant rice was so good that she ordered it every chance she got. The girls agreed to try the avocado green curry—a spicy dish—and both declared it a new favorite.

After dinner, Lucy volunteered to sweep up after the sander, and in the meantime, she could break down cardboard boxes that were stuffing up the tiny office and organize that space. Gracie agreed, and the girls set to work. Lucy carried several loads of flattened boxes to the recycling bin before she found the floor. The only boxes left were labeled as office supplies, so those she opened and put away on the shelves lining the room. There was an antique roll-top desk and a modern manager's chair in the room but nothing else in the way of furniture. As she dusted the shelves and swept up the floor, she noticed some deep scratches in the finish.

Gracie had just unplugged the sander when Lucy popped her head out and asked if she wanted to sand the office floor, too, since the sander was a rental that had to go back the next day. Gracie hadn't counted on being able to get to that cluttered space yet, so she came to see.

"Wow, Lucy. I can't believe it! Everything is so organized too!" Gracie leaned forward and kissed Lucy on both cheeks. "*Grazie, sorella!*"

Lucy smiled, bemused. "What does that mean?"

"It means 'thanks, sister!' in Italian."

"I thought you were Spanish?" Lucy was more confused than ever.

"I had one Italian grandmother who made sure I learned the language. She was very insistent, so my parents sent me to language classes, and I spent several summers in Italy."

Lucy was envious. She had always dreamed of sightseeing along the Mediterranean coast from Barcelona, Spain to Cannes in France, then Monaco, and finally, Livorno, Italy. She had a bucket list full of places she'd wanted to visit since she was a teenager and spent half the summer reading all the books in the travel section of her grandparents' bookstore.

"*Sorella* is such a beautiful word. I think it's from *soror* in Latin?" Lucy asked. "It's how we get 'sorority' in English."

"Yes, that's correct, Luce! You're such a brain!" Gracie winked at her. "It is a beautiful word. In fact, it gives me an idea. I was going to name the store Bella, for beautiful, but now maybe I will call it Bella Sorella—beautiful sister. What do you think?"

"I love it. Bella Sorella . . . it sounds magical!"

Together, Lucy and Gracie moved the desk out of the small room and pushed the chair out after it. Lucy wanted a turn with the sander, and Gracie was happy to let her have it, stating that her hands were a bit numb from doing the other floors.

As Lucy worked from one end of the small room to the other, her thoughts wandered to Mark and how much she missed him. She wondered if he would retire and take a job in the private sector or give in to the pressure and persuasion of higher-ups who used lucrative retention packages and promotions to keep him.

She was lost in thought when the drum sander hit something, creating sparks. The sparks landed on the fine wood sanding dust and started catching fire. Lucy shut the machine off and stamped the small flare-up. She moved the sander and discovered a nail head poking up just slightly from the floor. She checked the sander but didn't see any rips or tears in the belt.

Gracie poked her head into the room to investigate. Lucy pointed out the nail and told her what had happened. The smell of burning wood dust lingered in the air but the floor didn't appear to have suffered any burn marks.

Gracie decided to pull the nail rather than try to sink it below the surface of the wood. She grabbed a pry bar from her toolbox and popped it out. "That's blacksmith quality," she said.

The nail appeared to be hand-forged, with a tapered, square shaft and a rectangular wrought head.

"I'm sorry. I didn't see it. But I checked the sander out, and

I don't think it caused any damage. At least, I hope not. I'd feel terrible if I broke rented equipment!" Lucy tilted the sander up for Gracie to look.

"I think the sander is okay. I don't think I would have seen this nail either. The floor is pretty dark here. Let's check for any more nails, though, before we try again."

Both girls felt over the remaining floor where the desk had been situated. A few feet from where she hit the first nail, Lucy felt another. This one was barely protruding, sitting almost flush with the board. Gracie found two more nails a few feet away. Lucy realized the nails were in straight lines and across from each other in the shape of a square.

"Maybe we should leave the nails in and just pound them down?" Lucy said. "I'm afraid we'll damage something or cause the floor to cave in—"

"I've been under the building. The floor is stable and sturdy. There's nothing down there. Just cobwebs and plenty of storage space." Gracie pulled out another nail and rolled it in her palm. "These nails might be original, so I'll save them and probably put them back, but I think this might be a false floor. If so, who knows what kind of stuff could be in there. We need to at least check it out."

Lucy had an uneasy feeling about it, but she was curious too. After Gracie pried up all the nails, she pushed and poked in various places, but nothing shifted. Lucy tried standing in the middle of the square area and walking to one side and then the other, but again, nothing seemed loose. They used a screwdriver to try to wedge between two planks and lift one up, but the wood was too heavy or too well-secured in place.

After a few minutes, they gave up. Lucy could see Gracie was tired after a long day. "Go rest a few minutes and let me finish sanding the floors," she said. It wouldn't take long with the big floor sander.

Gracie agreed. "Hand-sanding the corners can wait for another day too."

Lucy made her first few passes over the remaining floor without finding more nail heads—but suddenly, the floor in front of her gave way. It swung inward in two pieces like shutters on a hinge. She managed to pull the sander back from the edge in the nick of time, keeping it and herself from being pulled into the newly opened hole. Her backward scramble ended with a crashing fall on her rump, though, and she let out a howl. "Ouch!"

Gracie came barreling into the room. "Lucy, are you okay? What happened?" Her eyes grew wide when she saw Lucy and the sander on the floor and then took in the large square hole. "*Dio mio!*"

She helped Lucy to her feet and checked her over. When Lucy insisted she was okay, they both crept to the edge of the hole.

"What did you do, Lucy? How did you open it?"

Lucy shook her head. "I don't think I did! I was sanding back and forth and had just touched on that part when the doors fell open. It was as if someone flipped a switch, and *bam*— they opened right up. Lucy hit the flashlight icon on her phone, using the beam to shine into the hole.

"There's a ladder over there," Gracie pointed to one end of the hole. A vertical, wooden ladder appeared to be fixed to the wall just below the floor. "I don't remember seeing this when I did my walk-through of the property with Sammy Sue, my agent, and we went everywhere down there. I would have remembered seeing something like that!"

"What were you doing just now? Before I fell, I mean." Lucy brushed as much wood dust as she could from her pants.

"Nothing, really. I was just messing around with the fireplace. The swinging arm attached to the wall of the fireplace seemed like it could be original to the building, too, so I swung it out and back in again to see how well it worked. Then I heard what sounded like a cannonball hit the floor."

Lucy rubbed her sore backside. "I guess I'm the cannonball! But in all fairness, the sander fell over with me!"

"I'm just glad you're okay," Gracie said. "If anything happened to you, I'd be really upset."

Lucy walked over to Gracie and gave her a warm hug. "And then you'd tease me about being a klutz forever, right?"

"Oh, I'm still gonna do that." Gracie winked.

"Why don't you go back out there and swing that arm again like you did before? I want to see if it closes." Lucy wanted to get to the bottom of the mysterious opening, but she wasn't sure she needed to get to the bottom of the floor. It was dark down there, and the ladder looked gray with dust and age.

Gracie tried swinging the arm in and out again a few times, but nothing happened. Lucy heard a clicking noise, but it was faint.

"I think maybe it has to be closed a different way," she called to her friend. *I just hope it isn't from inside.*

Lucy texted Sam to let him know where she was and what she was about to do—in case something happened. She also mentioned how the iron crane in the fireplace might have been what opened the access to the lower floor, just in case they ended up stuck down there with no way out. She didn't want to worry her grandparents, and she knew she could trust Sam to come looking for her if something happened.

Gracie had gone ahead of her down the ladder to see if there was a reason for Lucy to come down, and now she stood at the foot of the ladder, beckoning Lucy to hurry. "You're not going to believe this!"

Lucy chuckled to herself. If only Gracie knew! This wasn't her first rodeo with hidden spaces and buried surprises.

"Coming! I'm coming!"

She eased her way down the ladder. It had held Gracie's weight just fine, but Lucy was afraid it might not continue to hold. She jumped off before the final rungs and landed beside Gracie, who shone her flashlight in Lucy's eyes.

"Oh, sorry!" Gracie turned the light away when Lucy shielded her face. "Look at this! She illuminated the stone wall that lined one side of the space, which was wide enough for Lucy to spread her arms out to the sides. "This is the same wall I saw in the basement before. I didn't realize that basement wasn't as wide as the house. Someone walled up this space and then nailed it shut. I think the nails were pinning the hinges from opening, so no one ever knew this space was here."

She pointed overhead, where Lucy could just see the hinges that held the downward-swinging floorboards in place. That made sense to Lucy. Otherwise, the people who had lived or worked in the building over the years would have discovered it. The pins must have kept the fireplace lever from opening whatever mechanism latched the doors.

Lucy scanned the length of the chamber. It stayed about the same width from where they entered to the far end. It seemed to be about the length of the building above it, so maybe it was just a storage or hiding space they'd discovered.

Gracie felt along the stones of the long wall at the opposite end, pushing on them to see if any were loose. One stone wiggled in her hand, so she pulled it out and bent down to peer through.

"I can't see anything, but this should be the basement on the other side of the wall. I'm going to just barely put this stone back and look at it from the other side later." Gracie shimmied the stone about halfway back into its place and leaned up against the wall across from Lucy.

Everything happened at once. The wall Gracie leaned on gave way, and Gracie disappeared. The "floor doors" swung upward and latched together, plunging Lucy into darkness. Before she could react, she heard Gracie scream, but she wasn't screaming alone. There were at least two other voices that cried out in surprise. One of them, a female voice, started cursing in two languages.

Lucy decided to stay quiet and felt her way down the chamber to where she'd last seen her friend. She didn't want to pull her phone out yet and make her presence known. Her experience with people in tunnels and hidden spaces wasn't exactly helping calm her nerves.

Light flared beyond the gaping hole in the wall where Gracie disappeared. Lucy flattened her body against the wall next to the hole so that someone peering through might not see her. A woman—she was sure now that it wasn't Gracie—continued cursing and complaining.

"That's enough! You're okay. Be quiet, please!" A male voice echoed into the room, causing Lucy's heart to jump. She knew that voice!

"Sam! Is that you?"

"Lucy? Where are you?" Sam replied.

"I'm in here, just on the other side of the wall." Lucy's body was weak with relief. She pulled her cell phone from her back pocket and turned on the flashlight. She shined it into the opening but only saw a gaping void.

"Down here, Luce," Sam said.

She angled her beam toward the floor, surprised to see Sam's head a full story below. She swept her light around and caught Gracie lying on her side, holding her leg and covered in dust. Next to her, looking mad enough to spit nails, was Camilla, who appeared to have been knocked down by Gracie's fall. She was sitting up, though, and appeared to be unharmed at first glance.

"How did you know where to find me? I only sent the text a few minutes ago. How are you here, and, more importantly, where exactly are you? How did you get down there?" Lucy peppered Sam with questions. None of this made sense.

Sam glanced up at Lucy and then back down at the two women on the floor by his feet. "Lucy, I didn't get a text from you. We'll talk about the hows and whys later. Just tell me you have a way out up there? We're going to need an ambulance."

"I don't know if I can get out. The hatch we came through

closed when Gracie fell through the wall. I can climb the ladder and see if there's a way to open it, though." She held up her phone and peered at the screen. "I have bars! Gracie, are you okay? Just hang on. We'll get you out of here."

"What about me?" Cami whined. "This *la cretina* nearly killed me!"

Sam extended his hand to Cami, but she declined his assistance, so he bent over to check on Gracie, who hadn't said a word since the fall. He looked up at Lucy. "Maybe hurry, Luce."

Lucy returned to the ladder while dialing the number for Mark's father, Captain Andy Harrison. He'd always been quick to respond whenever she needed him, and this time was no different.

She explained where she was and how to open the hatch doors and asked him to call the fire rescue squad and an ambulance. He promised help was on the way. She debated a moment and then rang her grandmother's phone.

She explained everything. After asking multiple times if Lucy was really all right, her grandmother told her that Sam and Cami were in one of the tunnels that ran under the town. The town fathers had taken steps to brick up or close off all the access points to it, but she hadn't been aware that the chamber under the Trading Post connected to the tunnels below.

Lucy couldn't find a way to open the doors from below, so she ran back to check on the others. She wasn't sure how easy it would be for rescuers to haul Gracie up and out through the hole, through the narrow chamber, and then up again on the spindly ladder.

"Hang on, guys. Help is on the way." Lucy peered down into the tunnel, shining her light on each of them. Gracie was still cradling her leg but gave Lucy a tight-lipped nod. Her pain was palpable. Cami, now standing and leaning on Sam, just glared at her.

"I think I should go ahead a little way and see if I can find an easier way out of this tunnel." Sam looked up to Lucy, a question in his eyes.

"Yeah, I think that might be a good idea. It's going to be hard to pull everyone out from here, I think. Cami and I can stay here and watch Gracie." Lucy understood that Sam wanted to find an easier exit, but she thought he also had something else in mind. Perhaps he was curious to see if the tunnel connected to any others, especially any that might lead in the direction of Lucy's house.

"You can't leave me here alone!" Cami gripped Sam's arm harder.

"You're not alone. Lucy is right there, and Gracie too. Don't worry. I won't be gone long." Sam tried to disengage his arm.

"I will come with you. Maybe we should just go back the way we came." Cami had reattached her grip, as if trying to pull Sam away.

"You just said you couldn't walk two minutes ago. If you've injured your ankle, there's no way we could make it back the way we came. It's too steep and uneven. Just wait here. Lucy said help was coming." He snapped his arm free, and when it looked as if Cami was going to fall, he grabbed her around the waist and lowered her back to the floor.

"Just wait there, Cami. Captain Harrison will be here any minute. He'll know what to do." Lucy was aggravated with the woman who didn't seem to care at all that her friend was injured. She was willing to just go chasing off with Sam and leave Gracie alone, suffering in the dark.

"Fine!" Cami ground the words out but made her displeasure felt.

Sam gave Lucy a quick nod and headed farther down the tunnel with the light from his cell phone showing the way.

Maybe he'd find some other way out. If not, Lucy hoped that he'd find a dead end. The last thing she wanted was to discover there was another hidden way of accessing her family's home and property.

The minutes ticked by as Lucy felt powerless to help her friend, and Cami resorted to disregarding any attempt on Lucy's part to engage in conversation. She flat-out ignored everything Lucy said to her. Lucy kept her phone light trained on Gracie, who concentrated on breathing through the pain.

A metallic scraping sound and a puff of air on her back made Lucy turn to see that the hatch doors had opened, so she ran to the other end. Expecting to see a fireman or Captain Harrison, Lucy couldn't believe her eyes when a skinny leg that terminated in a house slipper appeared over the edge, searching for purchase on the ladder. A second leg joined the first and found a rung, and next, the hem of a familiar muumuu appeared as Lucy's grandmother lowered herself down.

Lucy climbed up a couple of rungs and put her arms up as a guard in case Glo were to fall. "What are you doing here?"

"I came to make sure you were okay. I thought you might need some company."

Her grandmother looked innocent enough, but Lucy was sure there was more to it than concern for her welfare.

"So, you didn't come to get a look at the hidden chamber or the tunnel?" Lucy smiled, already knowing the answer. "Sam has gone farther down the tunnel to see if he can find an easier way in for the rescue squad, and Cami is sitting down there with Gracie. I think Gracie is pretty banged up, so I hope they get here soon."

"Lucy, are you down there?" A male voice called from the room above.

"Yes, over here!" Lucy shouted.

A face appeared over the edge of the opening, but it wasn't Captain Harrison or one of the rescuers. It was Sam. He was covered in muck and appeared to be bleeding.

"Lucy, this is bad—" He cut off his words when he noticed her grandmother standing behind her. "Glo, what are you doing here? Never mind, you need to get up here."

"Are you okay? What happened?" Lucy asked.

Sam gestured to the blood on his sleeve and front. "I'm fine. It isn't what you think."

"But what about Gracie and Cami? I can't just climb up and leave them down there alone." Lucy shook her head. "How did you get here before Andy?"

"Just come up here, Luce, and you too, Mrs. Patterson. There's something you need to know. Don't worry about Cami and Gracie. The paramedics are almost there. I found another way in."

Glo started up the ladder, but Lucy hesitated. Sam helped the older woman the rest of the way and ensured she was on her feet before turning back to Lucy.

"Lucy, I found a way out, but that's not all I found. I tripped over something. It turned out to be a body—Cami's father. She doesn't know."

Chapter Thirteen

Sam took a deep breath. "The tunnel branches off, and the branch I followed empties into the sewer. It looked like it had been bricked over in the past but had crumbled, and I was able to just walk out and open the grate. I came out near the road and called Andy. He notified and diverted everyone to the sewer entrance. They'll be able to roll Gracie out and lift her from the drain a lot easier. The EMTs will keep them both there until they can cover the body and secure the crime scene.

"Andy sent me around this way to bring you out, Lucy. He'll tell Cami about her father once she gets checked out at the hospital." Sam backed up as Lucy shot up the ladder.

She could hear the paramedics below as they arrived and began to triage the two women.

"What do you mean by 'crime scene,' Sam? Couldn't it have just been natural causes or an accident?" Lucy shuddered. Poor Cami. It was true that she didn't much care for Cami, but to move to a new place and lose a family member wasn't something she would have wished on anyone.

"No, it's not possible." Sam shuddered. "I don't want to think about it."

"I don't understand. What were you and Cami doing down there in the first place?" Lucy was piqued. She felt a little betrayed, after all they'd been through together, that he hadn't called her the minute he'd found some sort of tunnel.

"Cami called me from the church. She said she couldn't find her father and asked me to come up there and look around with her. The church can be kind of creepy after dark."

Lucy nodded. She knew that was true. Once, as a teenager, she'd snuck out to go swimming with some of the locals, and they'd spent the night sleeping on pews afterward because she was afraid to go back to her grandparents' house. The church was never locked, at least not the sanctuary. She'd woken up in the early morning hours feeling as if someone was watching her, and she was pretty sure that someone wasn't God.

"We looked all over, starting in the parsonage and then the church. We checked the attics and the crawl spaces, closets—pretty much everywhere. Then we went down to the basement and found the door to the vault open."

"We have a vault under the church? Like a crypt?" Lucy felt uneasy at the idea that she'd just been singing familiar hymns while standing over someone's final resting place.

Glo shot Lucy an impatient look. "Yes, but no one has been entombed there for at least a hundred years. Let Sam continue." She nodded for him to go on.

"We went in, and one of the crypts was open, but it wasn't a crypt. It was a passageway. Cami was worried that her father had gone in and gotten hurt, so we started making our way down. It was a man-made shaft at first, but it connected to a stone tunnel. It kept going downhill, so we followed it. I wanted to call for help before we went in too far, but Cami didn't want to lose any more time in case her father was injured.

"When we came to the level part of the tunnel, it seemed like it would just keep going and going, but her father wasn't where we thought he would be if he'd fallen. We were just about to head back up the tunnel when a bunch of dirt came down from overhead, followed by some stones—and then Gracie. I think she hit the ground and rolled into Cami. Then you appeared, Lucy, so you know the rest."

"You kids have had quite the adventure, and it's getting pretty late. Why don't I drop you home, Sam? Lucy, you can ride home with me. We can pick up your car tomorrow." Glo seemed agitated. "If Andy wants to get a statement from either of you, he can see you in the morning."

"Shouldn't we go to the hospital? I don't want to just leave Gracie. I think she's pretty badly injured." Lucy nodded to Sam. "He probably wants to check on Cami too. She'll need a ride home from the hospital."

"I think it might be better if you both stepped back from your new friends for just a bit. They're strangers, and strange things are going on. People are messing around where they shouldn't. And now, we have a killer on the loose." Glo put one hand on her hip, defying them to argue.

Sam and Lucy hotly contested the idea that their friends had anything to do with it, but Glo wasn't listening. She turned and walked out of the back room toward the front door. "Turn off the lights and lock the door on your way out. You can text Gracie and tell her not to worry about the store. Oh, and you may want to yank that iron crane back so the doors close. That way, no one can get in from below."

"That didn't seem to work before," Lucy said. "I couldn't figure out any way to close them. In fact, I'm not sure what made them close." *Or who.*

"Just swing it in and out three times, one right after the other. That'll do it." Glo opened the door to leave. "And hurry up. I'll be waiting in the car."

Glo had driven Sam to the church to pick up his car. He didn't argue, but Lucy could see by the determined look in his eyes that he planned to rush straight to the hospital. He was a caring and compassionate person, she knew, but it seemed that his concern for Cami was more than just that of a friend. He'd fallen for her and fallen hard. Lucy wanted him to be happy, but she didn't think Cami was the right person for Sam. Still, Sam seemed blind to the woman's faults.

As soon as Sam was out of the car, Lucy turned to her grandmother. It was time for some answers.

"So, you knew about the hidden chamber under the Trading Post? I mean, obviously, you did since you knew how to open and close it." Lucy tugged at her seatbelt in the passenger's side of her grandmother's car.

"I've never seen it, but I knew it existed. It's been boarded up since before I was born. I didn't know that it intersected one of the tunnels. In fact, I wonder if it did in the beginning. I think it's possible that part of the tunnel roof caved in at some point, leaving just a thin layer of earth between the stone foundation and the tunnel. It's a wonder the whole building didn't collapse, as old as it is. But yes, I read about the clever hiding spot and how to access it in one of the journals. It wasn't supposed to be able to open now, though."

"It worked now because we removed some nails. I think they were jamming the hinge pins so they wouldn't move even if someone played with the fireplace crane." A thought occurred to Lucy. "What journals?"

Glo drove around the curves of the hillside like a race car driver, hugging the inside lane like a pro. Lucy thought her grandmother would fit in perfectly at the Monaco Grand Prix—zipping around the winding track in Monte Carlo should be a breeze.

"We have records, journals that go back a way. The first journal is from the days when our family had the rancho here. Every generation after that has added to the collection. They kept a record of what was found and where and how they managed to keep possession of the property even when governments changed hands. Some of them talked about the things that washed up in various places and about creating tunnels and walling off access to caves. Your great-great-grandparents were the first to share the burden with a few trusted friends, and it was their vision to use some of the accumulated wealth to benefit the town. That's where the secret circle began."

"Why have I never seen these journals? It really feels as if you don't trust me. When we thought you and Grandpa were gone, I did everything I thought you'd want me to do. I went into it blind, though. I had no idea what was really going on or the secrets you guys were keeping from me. Why are you trying to push me out now?" A lump formed in Lucy's throat, and her eyes burned with hot, unshed tears. It felt as if her grandparents were rejecting her, and it hurt.

"The journals are locked away in one of the compass rooms for safekeeping." Her grandmother referred to the four rooms in the cellar of the house, each facing a different direction. "And I'm sorry for what you went through. Having you suffer, thinking we were dead and not knowing what happened, and then being threatened and attacked—well, that's the last thing we wanted. We've tried to ensure you and your parents were protected, no matter what, but sometimes things don't go to plan. You need to understand: it was supposed to be many years from now that you'd find everything out. We wanted you to have a happy, normal life for as long as possible."

"So why try to keep me out of it now?" Lucy still didn't understand. "The cat is out of the bag; the horse is out of the barn. There's really no going back."

"We didn't tell your father until you were grown. We didn't want him to live under the shadow of it either. He didn't really want anything to do with it, and he didn't want us to tell you either. He and your mother decided to take a portion of what would eventually have been their inheritance and use it to help people. We set up the trust to come to you next, but we didn't intend for that to happen so soon. We're just afraid that now too many people know or suspect something. Always before, it stayed in the circle. Hattie, Doctor Wilson, Big Sam, even Fuchsia Butterfield. They were all the grandchildren of the original circle of friends. Even me. My grandparents were part of the original circle."

Lucy didn't know what to say. Her grandmother pulled into the driveway and eased toward the dark house. She hoped her grandfather was asleep.

"Part of my concern, Lucy, is that the original circle has pretty much dispersed or died off. There's only young Sam to help you look after things. Fuchsia and Hattie never had children. Larry—Dr. Wilson—decided to keep it from his sons, who moved away. And I know he didn't plan to tell his foster daughter and her husband."

Lucy recalled Dr. Wilson sending his son-in-law, Allen Morgan, to install a security system for the house and bookstore. At the time, she had no idea herself what the house hid in its walls and underneath. If he'd known anything about it, he hadn't let on.

"What about Mark, though? He's like a son to Hattie. And he means a great deal to me." Lucy was grateful for everything Mark had done to help and protect her, and he'd kept the secret, as well.

Glo sighed. "It's regrettable that he knows. I'm thankful he helped you. I'll always be thankful for that. But he's an unknown factor, really. His mother's character was questionable at best. I know Hattie thinks the world of him and that you do as well, but we're very accustomed to keeping things close to the chest, not sharing it outside of the circle. We don't know where this relationship is going between the two of you. What happens if you have a bad breakup? He works for the government too. Maybe a sense of duty kicks in, and he feels obligated to report what he knows—which, thankfully, isn't everything. And now it turns out that Andy Harrison is his father. That's all we need . . . for the local police to find out. It couldn't be much worse!"

Lucy opened the door and climbed out of the car. She looked up to see the sky blazing with diamond-like stars. Their beauty took her breath away. "I don't think you're giving Mark enough credit. He would never betray me or this family." She was sure of it. Deep down in her bones, she knew that she knew.

"Maybe so. I hope not. I always thought maybe you and young Sam would end up together."

Lucy rolled her eyes. Sam was great, but they were better as friends.

Her grandmother locked the car and walked with Lucy up the steps. "I'm worried, Lucy. And after tonight, I think I have every right to be. I don't want to push you out, but I'll do whatever I must to keep you safe."

*T*or, the best bookstore cat ever by all accounts, lay purring in a shaft of sunlight on the desk. Lucy was there first, but the feline had gradually pushed her to one corner of the desk where she now balanced her laptop. The local paper had gone digital, and she was starved for news.

After taking her statement, Captain Andy Harrison had only told her that she and Gracie were lucky to be alive, considering the age and condition of the building. He warned her to stay out of places she shouldn't be because he didn't want to see her get hurt like her friend had been. It was a miracle Gracie only had a sprain and some cuts and bruises. She'd been released the next day, and one of the junior officers had taken her home.

Lucy went by the store to check on Gracie's car a couple of times while she was laid up at home. The store itself was surrounded by caution tape and had a No Entry notice on the door. Until the building inspector and the head of public works for the city signed off, it would have to remain closed.

Lucy had only seen Gracie once since the accident. She'd driven out to the rural retreat center to Gracie's leased cabin with two bags full of freezer meals from Hattie. Gracie was happy to see Lucy and thrilled with the food delivery, but she was visibly in enough pain that Lucy didn't want to stay long.

Lucy had tried reaching out to Sam, but he was despondent and didn't want to talk. He'd gone to the hospital to check on Cami, but she refused to see him. She'd been physically fine from Gracie falling on her, but upon being given the news about her father's death and why it was being treated as a homicide, she'd fainted and hit her head while still in the hospital's ED. They kept her for observation after doing tests and clearing her from anything worse than a knot on her scalp. Since then, she'd ghosted Sam and refused to answer the door whenever anyone stopped by the parsonage to check on her.

Lucy's grandparents were out for the afternoon, leaving her to run the store and tend to Tor's aggressive needs for treats and chin scritches. She enjoyed the quiet—only a few people had come in to browse, and none needed help with anything—but her mind was spinning.

She had asked her grandparents about the crypt and tunnel leading from the church, but they weren't very forthcoming. They admitted knowing there was such a thing but implicated that no one alive, outside of their circle, would have known about it.

The church itself hid some of the evidence of the earliest history of Seaview. Parts of it were built with wood reclaimed from the shipwreck of the Spanish treasure galleon. All this time, it was hiding in plain sight. The man-made tunnel connected with a natural lava tube that led to the shore, and buccaneers and bandits used it at various times until the church construction. Engineers eventually walled off the tunnel to build storm sewers for the growing town.

Both her grandparents had been on edge since the vault discovery. The police hadn't come up with a motive for the pastor's killing, and so far, they'd kept the details a closely guarded secret. The EMTs and other first responders had rescued the women and removed the body from a natural cavern that had been sealed up behind the storm sewers long ago—end of story. They hadn't been told how anyone had arrived there.

Sam, Gracie, Lucy, and her grandparents had all agreed not to share the details until the investigation was over. Cami had given her statement to the officers at the hospital and then secluded herself away from everyone. The church was closed off during the investigation, but the crypt details were barred from the public too. Lucy's grandmother insisted it was just a matter of time before someone started figuring things out and reviving interest in the rumors. And that could lead to problems.

Lucy clicked the refresh button on her browser. The editor of the Seaview Review sometimes put out updates late in the afternoon when something notable happened, and a murdered pastor fit that description.

She was rewarded with a fresh article about the case—this time with a photo. She scanned it, but there wasn't anything new. Just an appeal from the police for information. She clicked on the photo. It was a candid shot of Humble Delacruz talking to someone in the church hall. She wasn't sure who the shorter man in a casual jacket was. Lucy zoomed in on the pastor's face, searching his features for something she couldn't put her finger on. He looked unhappy in the photo, but she couldn't tell if it was his natural resting face or if he was displeased with what he was hearing.

She wished she knew more about him, but he wasn't a social media user, and an online search turned up nothing she didn't already know. She wondered why the editor had chosen this picture. It wasn't a good choice if something formal or higher quality had been available. That likely meant Cami hadn't supplied it. Maybe one of the church members sent it in. She clicked out to see if there was a photo credit, but none was listed.

Tor stretched, aiming to take over the last corner of the desk. When the laptop didn't budge, he rolled over and put his paws on the keyboard, resting his head as if the computer were his personal pillow. Lucy inched the laptop out from under him and conceded the desk. When she settled at the dining room table, though, she realized Tor had clicked something.

The dialog window asked if she'd like to search the image, and that gave her an idea. She zoomed and cropped the picture to include just the pastor's head and shoulders, then she hit search. It might not come up with anything, but facial recognition technology was always improving.

A few dozen photos popped up as possible matches. Some were easy to eliminate—they were older or deceased already—but a few looked very much the same. The problem was the name, though. Lucy had hoped to find more information on Humble Delacruz. However, she kept finding pictures of his face belonging to a man named Pedro Alvarez, who was listed as a professor of antiquities at the University of Valencia in Spain.

Her stomach twisted in knots. Maybe she was wrong and Pastor Delacruz only looked like the man in the pictures. Or perhaps he was a relative. Everyone has a double somewhere in the world, wasn't that the saying? But what were the odds that the murdered man would be a doppelganger for someone whose area of expertise related to her own family's secret?

She closed her computer and stood up. No one was in the bookstore now, so she locked the door and turned over a sign: Back in Thirty Minutes. Her mind raced. She needed to tell her grandparents and Sam. She needed to tell the police. She wanted to tell Mark, but he wouldn't have a day off until tomorrow. So, she decided to tell the cat.

"Tor, we've got a problem."

In the end, Lucy called and left a voicemail for Mark. Her grandparents weren't quite ready to trust him, but Lucy trusted no one more. She plucked the keys from her grandmother's hiding spot in the antique desk. The treasures once hidden there had been removed for safekeeping, and she didn't know where they were now.

She had to be quick to succeed in her mission because her grandparents could return at any time. Lucy sprinted down the stairs to the basement, where she was shocked to find that each of the four doors had stacks of heavy furniture and boxes placed in front of them. With enough time, it wouldn't stop someone who wanted to get in there, but it was an effective deterrent for Lucy. She wondered if her grandparents didn't trust her, or if they had arranged things this way in case intruders found their way into the house again.

Instead of returning upstairs, Lucy wandered over to the side of the basement that led to the root cellar. Hidden passageways could be accessed from the root cellar if someone knew how. Lucy had learned all about them earlier in the summer when she'd found her grandfather there in bad shape from rough treatment at the hands of his abductors.

The door to the root cellar was not covered up as usual, which seemed odd. She raised the inset handle and swung the door upward until it was fully extended and then felt her way down the first few steps until she could reach the light. Various things were stored in crates and boxes and neatly on shelves, leaving the impression that the space was organized and used for long-term storage. Lucy scanned the room. She hadn't been down here since Mark and Doctor Wilson helped carry her grandfather up the stairs and back to safety.

One side of the room had a hidden panel that opened to reveal a staircase that ran from the top of the Victorian to the bottom and even to a level beneath the root cellar. No one would ever guess it was there looking at it. On the opposite side, a long set of shelves lined the wall. Lucy noticed that the shelves were pulled away from the wall on one side, as they had been the first time she'd explored the room.

Behind those shelves was a stone wall with circular depressions that seemed to make a meaningful pattern. But spending a lot of energy pressing on them and looking for ways to make that wall move had accomplished nothing. In the end, she'd decided it was just a diversion to fool anyone who might come looking for the actual passageway. She had found a small scrap of paper with a single word written on it—Illuminate—behind the shelves, but she'd never managed to figure out what it was for.

Curiosity aroused, Lucy crossed the room and swung the bookshelf farther away from the wall. She yelped and dropped her phone. Cami lay behind the bookshelf, unmoving.

Chapter
Fifteen

This is bad. Lucy leaned over and retrieved her phone. She shone the light on Cami's face, but her eyes were closed. The light caught the breathing movement as Cami's chest rose and fell. Relief flooded Lucy—at least the woman wasn't dead! That's the last thing anyone needed.

But how had she gotten in the house, and how had she ended up behind the bookshelf in the root cellar? Lucy wondered if the woman was playing possum, so she used the toe of her shoe to nudge Cami's foot and said, "Get up, Cami! This isn't funny! I'm going to call the police!"

Cami didn't budge or react in any way, so Lucy ran back to the stairs and up to the basement, where she had a better signal.

She dialed Hattie's number first because she knew her grandparents were planning an early dinner at the Lace Curtain Café. Hattie picked up on the second ring.

"Lucy, where have you been, my girl? I miss you!" Hattie's cheerful nature and kind words came through the phone like a hug.

"Hattie, are my grandparents there?"

"Yes, they're out the back having a cozy dinner under the filbert tree. Is everything okay?" So, the older woman had cottoned on to the fact that Lucy was anxious.

"Well, not really. I need you to discreetly ask them to come home quickly, but without making any kind of scene. We have a, uh, problem at the house." Lucy bit her lip and debated whether she should tell Hattie any more than that.

"Okay, Lucy, will do. Do you need anything else? I can take a break any time. Hector has everything under control here."

"Yes, if you don't mind, pick up Doctor Wilson. We're going to need him, but it's better if I don't tell you why over the phone. Just have him bring his bag."

"You're not hurt, are you?" Hattie asked.

"No, I'm fine. Just tell my grandparents to hurry."

Lucy debated what to do. She wasn't sure she wanted to return to Cami, but she didn't want to leave her unattended. If someone had done this to her, they might still be in the house. Was it possible that other people knew about the tunnels and were lying in wait? If Cami was faking being unconscious, Lucy couldn't tell. She didn't want to take any chances in case the woman turned on her. She felt stuck as she stood just inside the basement door, one hand with a death grip on the handrail.

Before she could gather the courage to go down to Cami or out to wait for her grandparents, she heard a noise at the back door. Someone tapped softly, then rattled the door as they checked to see if it was unlocked. The hair rose on her arms. It couldn't be her grandparents. It was too fast, and they would have come in the front door with their keys. She eased down a stair, hoping to close the door behind her before anyone had a chance to break in and discover her there.

She heard another knock, louder this time, followed by a muffled voice calling through the door.

"Lucy? Can you hear me? Are you okay?"

Relief flooded her body, causing her knees to nearly give way. She scrambled back up the stairs and into the kitchen on shaky legs to unlock the back door.

"Mark! How?" She let herself fall forward into his waiting arms.

Lucy sat in a kitchen chair, hands wrapped around a hot cup of tea. Mark, her grandparents, and Dr. Wilson were all downstairs assessing Cami. Hattie sat across from Lucy, stirring honey into her own cup. Everyone had arrived together just a few minutes after Mark, who'd explained to Lucy that he'd found someone to cover the last of his shift. Her voicemail about what she'd discovered on the heels of the murder worried him enough that he was on his way not long after he checked his messages. Lucy was thankful because she wasn't sure her grandparents and their "seasoned" friends would be able to handle the situation if a killer was on the loose somewhere on the property.

Dr. Wilson came up first. He nodded in the affirmative. "She's going to be okay. We'll bring her upstairs and put her on the back patio."

Mark, with a still-unconscious Cami in his arms, appeared next and followed Dr. Wilson out the back door. They arranged Cami on the outdoor sofa, making it appear as if she were sleeping.

Her grandmother came up next and sat at the table with Hattie and Lucy.

"We called the non-emergency number and told them that Cami was here—that she was passed out on the patio and looked as if she was sleeping off a bender. I talked to Andy. The story is that Lucy saw her and called us, then Hattie called and picked up the doctor on their way. No one was worried until she didn't wake up, which is when Dr. Wilson called for EMS. Everything is true except where you found her." She quirked an eyebrow at Lucy. "We don't want them to know she was in the house. It's just better that way. Doc says she appears to have been dosed with something, but her vitals are stable."

Lucy felt uneasy. She didn't like lying, and especially hated the idea of lying to the police. Never mind that Captain Harrison was also Mark's father. "What if she wakes up and remembers where she really was?" Lucy rubbed her head to dispel the pressure building up behind her forehead. "What if whoever did this is still here?"

"Don't worry about that. Your grandad is making sure everything is locked up tight and inaccessible. As soon as Cami leaves for the hospital, we'll check the passages, but I'm pretty sure whoever did this is gone." Her grandmother patted her hand. "Can you stick to the story? It's safer for everyone if we don't involve any more people."

Lucy glanced out the kitchen window, where Mark was waiting with the doctor. "I can stick to the story, but I will need you to start telling me the truth. No more shutting me out. And Mark is part of the package. I trust him, and you're going to have to trust him. Hattie trusts him, Doctor Wilson trusts him, and if Sam were here, he'd say the same. Mark is part of the circle, and so am I. Deal?"

Lucy looked her grandmother in the eye. She was done being left in the dark and excluded because her grandparents felt knowing things would put her in danger. They needed to realize that she wasn't going anywhere and was as determined to keep them safe as they were to keep her safe.

Ulyss came into the kitchen and stood behind Lucy's chair, putting one hand on her shoulder. Her grandfather's thinness continued to worry Lucy, but his grip was firm.

"You're right, Lucy. You and Mark have proven that you can take care of yourselves and that you're both trustworthy." He inclined his head to the now closed and locked basement door.

"Everything is as it should be," he said. Lucy's grandmother looked at him for a moment before nodding.

"Okay then," she said.

Lucy couldn't believe it. Just like that, her grandmother had changed her tune. Oh well, it was about time!

Hattie stood and stretched her shoulders. "I think it's for the best. In fact, I think it's long overdue. And seeing how trouble keeps turning up, I think it's time we talk about the future. Things have changed, and it's going to get harder and harder to keep everyone safe—and keep the secrets too." She came around the table and kissed Lucy on the head. "The future belongs to the young. It's not our world anymore."

Lucy's grandmother stiffened as Hattie spoke, but then her shoulders slumped as she considered her words.

"It's true, and enough people have been hurt already. I certainly don't want certain burdens to be passed on to Lucy and to her children. Maybe it's time to start the clock." Glo smiled up at her husband. "What do you think, Ulyss? Is it time for light to shine in the darkness?"

A great, heavy sigh worked its way out of Lucy's grandfather. "I don't think we have a choice. But first, we have to safeguard things from whoever is behind this." He waved a hand to where Cami was being loaded onto a stretcher in the backyard. "Nobody's safe until we figure out who killed Cami's father and who knocked her out in our root cellar."

Lucy realized that she hadn't shared her discovery with anyone but Mark yet. "About that. There's something I need to show you." She pulled up her laptop and opened the pictures she'd been looking at earlier. "Cami's father wasn't who he said he was. Which means we have no idea who she is either."

Dr. Wilson left with the ambulance, and Mark returned through the back door with his father following behind.

Police Captain Andy Harrison glared at the assembled group. "Somebody needs to start explaining now. Mark told me everything."

Lucy couldn't believe it. Her grandparents were starting to trust Mark. How could he betray her and her family that way? She looked up, hoping for some sort of answer from Mark, but his face was blank, giving her no indication one way or the other. Had he broken down and told his father that they'd moved Cami outdoors? Or that the house was riddled with secret passages and covered a much older system of tunnels and rooms? She swallowed her fear—and a painful lump in her throat—before she answered.

"I don't know anything more than what Mark told you. I saw her outside asleep on the patio, and I supposed that she was passed out from drinking because she was grieving her father. So, I called my grandparents at Hattie's. They came home, and Hattie picked up Doctor Wilson on the way here. Was that wrong? Should I have called for the ambulance straight away? I really didn't want to upset her more if she was just sleeping off a bender." Lucy felt a little sick, but she kept a straight face.

Captain Harrison's face softened. "No, Lucy, that was okay. Mark told me that you suspect Cami's father was not who he said he was. I can tell you that's true, but I need to know how you know that. We haven't released that information to the public. And why would Cami come here? Were you friends with her?"

Lucy didn't hesitate to answer. "We were *not* friends. She didn't like me very much, but I'm not sure why."

"And why did you think the pastor was not who he claimed?" Andy's voice was very soft, and his eyes seemed to be pleading with her to have a good answer.

"No reason, really. I saw his picture in the paper and decided to look him up on social media. But when I did a reverse image search, his face kept coming up with a different name. It could be a coincidence, but it sure seemed like him."

"Why didn't you call me?" Andy asked. "If you know something like that, you should share it with us. If you don't, it hinders an investigation."

"Well, I didn't know for sure, and it was just earlier this afternoon that I found the pictures and had questions about them . . . That was right before all this . . ." She waved her hand in the direction of the basement door, but Andy didn't seem to notice her faux pax. "Before I saw Cami."

"Well, you were right. Pastor Humble Delacruz doesn't exist. His real name is Pedro Alvarez." Andy made eye contact with each of them. "Is there anything else I need to know?"

Lucy volunteered. "He may have been a professor of antiquities from Valencia, Spain."

Andy smiled at her. "Good work, Lucy. He was, at one time. According to Interpol, however, he's also a thief and a smuggler specializing in relics from the Iberian Peninsula. Now we just need to figure out why he was here in Seaview. We're a long way from Portugal and Spain."

The knot was back in her stomach.

Mark insisted that Lucy take the rest of the day off with him, and her grandparents were happy to agree. They closed the bookstore early—no one felt like dealing with potential customers after all the drama earlier in the afternoon.

Daylight hours were growing shorter, so Lucy was happy to grab a warm jacket and head out for a walk with Mark. They set out toward town and were rewarded with displays of fall blooms and autumn decorations on every street. All the businesses were gearing up for the big Fall Festival in two weeks.

First, however, the annual Sea Glass Festival was scheduled to open on the beach and boardwalk. Lucy looked forward to it. There seemed to be no end to the creative works of art people made from sea glass. She had a running list of things she wanted to buy—a necklace for Hattie in pastel rainbow colors, some turquoise blue earrings for her grandmother, and one of those adorable sea glass Christmas trees she'd seen advertised online. Mark had the weekend off, so they planned to spend at least one day enjoying the festival together.

She breathed in the scent of pumpkin spice cinnamon rolls as they passed Honey's Bakery. She made a mental note to come back for a whole box of those later. Carbs don't count if they have pumpkin in the ingredients. She was sure of it.

She tucked her hand through Mark's elbow and laid her head on his arm. He leaned down to kiss her on the head but missed and kissed the top of her ear. She didn't care where it landed. She was just thrilled he was there—and kissing *her*. She'd seen a few of the looks other women threw in her direction when she was with Mark, and she knew more than one of them would be happy to trade places with her.

"Do you want to stop for a drink?" Mark asked. "The coffee shop is still open."

"I'm happy to wait for dinner. Unless you want something?"

"Nah, I'm good for now." Mark pointed toward the bluffs overlooking the ocean. Looks like we're going to have a beautiful sunset. Do you want to walk down to the park and watch?"

"Sounds perfect."

The sky was a smashed palette of pink and coral and rose gold, with shimmery clouds like feathers dipped in paint. As the sun began to dip below the steely gray horizon of the Pacific, the wind blew Lucy's hair up, fanning it out in waves behind her.

"Lucy, is that you?"

Lucy turned to see who was calling her from the parking area. She was delighted to see it was Gracie, who was waving with one hand and holding on to her car with the other. She had a stack of takeout containers on her hood and a crutch under her arm. Lucy waved back. She was so happy to see her friend out and about after her injury. Gracie started to say something else, but she wobbled, and her crutch shot out from under her arm.

In mere seconds, Mark jumped up, ran across the grass, and managed to catch Gracie before she hit the ground. He helped her back to her feet and retrieved the crutch for her.

Lucy followed him over, impressed with his speed and reflexes but concerned about her friend.

She reached Gracie and hugged her and then kept a protective arm around her waist.

"Don't scare me like that!" Lucy teased her friend.

"You? I scared myself even more!" Gracie laughed. "Thank you, kind sir. You are a knight in shining armor!" She winked at Lucy. "Is he always this gallant?"

"Absolutely! Mark Fellows, meet Graciela Jimenez. Mark is a Coast Guard captain, and Gracie here just bought the old McCoy's Trading Post to open a new store." She squeezed Gracie and let her go now that she was sure she had her balance. "Mark is my—"

"Boyfriend. I'm her boyfriend. Nice to meet you, Miss Jimenez." Mark gave her a warm smile.

"And Gracie is my new—" Lucy started to add.

"BFF? Gal pal? Partner in scary adventures?" Gracie laughed.

"I was going to say, 'new, wonderful friend.'" Lucy grabbed her hair and put it in a loose bun to stop the flyaways from getting in her eyes. "I think we've had enough scary adventures, right?"

Gracie pulled a scrunchie off her wrist and handed it to Lucy, who gratefully took it and wrapped it around her bun.

Mark watched the two women with a hint of a smile. "How about I take my best girl and her new best friend out for dinner? Have you eaten yet, Gracie?"

"I haven't," she said. "I did pick up some dessert from the bakery to munch on this week. Honey's had a cinnamon roll cheesecake I couldn't pass up."

Lucy's stomach gurgled. Honey's Bakery was famous for unique treats and special holiday confections found nowhere else.

"I think Lucy is a yes, if her growling stomach has anything to say about it." Mark wrapped an arm around her shoulder and winked. "What do you say, Gracie? Do you like Thai food?"

"You don't have to ask me twice. I love Thai. I wasn't looking forward to going home to eat alone for sure—I've had cabin fever all week!"

"I'm up for some Thai. I've been craving pumpkin curry all week." Lucy walked around to the passenger side door of Gracie's car. "Mark, I'll go with Gracie, and we'll follow you out there." She turned to Gracie and said, "It's kind of tucked away, easy to miss."

Mark, in mock outrage, said, "I know you both just want to gossip about me! Fine. Whatevs." Both women laughed. They laughed even harder as he pretended to sashay back to his truck.

The morning of the sea glass festival started off right. The sky was a stunning blue populated with perfect, fluffy white clouds scattered around evenly. Lucy almost felt like she was in a Pixar movie with the perfect, animated background. The light breeze was delicious and cool, but the day promised to be mild and comfortable.

Mark planned to meet Lucy for an early breakfast before they headed out for the day, so she showered and dressed at top speed. She pulled on a cream tank top and layered a bohemian peasant blouse over it, pairing it with tan cargo-style pants. The pants were perfect for the day—they'd hide sand and dirt, plus they were designed to roll up to be capris for wading. They also had hidden zippers at the knee to transform into walking shorts, too, if the temperatures soared.

She slipped on a comfortable pair of sandals, pulled her hair up into a loose side pony, and tossed sunblock, lip gloss, sunglasses, and a wide-brimmed hat in her market bag. Lucy was ready to go a little bit early, so she walked down the hall to her grandparents' room. She was about to knock when her grandmother's voice made her pause.

"I don't think we can trust her. I'm pretty sure she was snooping around when we were out. I don't want to confront her yet because we don't have proof—the security cameras were conveniently not working. I tell you, she's up to something!"

Heartbroken, Lucy slipped away down the hall and out the front door. Okay, maybe she had gone downstairs to see what she could find out. But she thought they were past it and willing for her to be involved and not kept in the dark any longer. She couldn't make her grandparents trust her, but now she wondered if she could trust them. Had it all been a show when they agreed to include her and Mark in the inner circle?

"Right. I'm not going to let this bother me. Too much drama." She made her way downstairs, fed Tor, and left through the front door, remembering to set the alarm and lock the door as she went. She wondered how on earth Cami had ended up in the root cellar since no alarm had ever gone off, and someone was always around when to store was open.

The alarm system was still new, installed by Dr. Wilson's son-in-law over the summer after both Lucy and an elderly woman were attacked. Lucy's grandparents must have activated the video components since their return. The cameras only covered the front door and the interior of the bookstore, so if someone broke in through the back or, heaven forbid, one of the tunnels beneath, the video cameras wouldn't have picked it up anyway.

Lucy had learned that Dr. Wilson had two sons, but he and his wife had fostered a young woman from the community. Though she was never legally adopted, they considered her their daughter and her husband like a son.

Lucy parked in one of the only remaining spaces adjacent to the Lace Curtain Café and put her sunglasses on her head. Dazzling light danced on the water, and gentle offshore breakers flashed a beautiful shade of green before the waves fell into foam.

She looked forward to spending the day watching the waves as she shopped for sea glass treasures.

Hattie's café was absolutely hopping. There was a line out the front door waiting for indoor seating, and a second hostess station had been set up outside in the front garden for outdoor tables. Hattie's crew had added card tables with patio umbrellas, but every table was full. Hattie had even invited a couple of breakfast food trucks to park in her parking lot for the morning rush. Lucy pulled out her phone to call Mark. Maybe he'd want to go someplace else, considering the crowds and growing chaos. Before she could dial, her favorite teen waiter, Kai, came over and took her aside.

"Lucy! Is this crazy, or what? Hattie told me to look out for you. I'll take you to your friends." Kai pulled her to move past the waiting crowds, earning her a couple of aggravated looks.

"Oh, I'm not meeting friends. I'm supposed to meet Mark here for a breakfast date." She felt the warmth of a flush flood her cheeks.

"You'll see. Just come on."

Lucy followed Kai into the sideyard, supposing they were headed for the back garden, but he stopped to open the wooden gate that led to Hattie's private patio. Lucy had only been back there once or twice for iced tea and a visit. It was her private sanctuary, Lucy knew, so she was surprised Kai was taking her into it.

"Make yourself comfortable. Hattie will be out in a minute." Kai motioned for Lucy to go on in.

Hattie had redecorated—the entire space was a sort of bohemian paradise. She'd hung gauzy fabric from an iron birdcage trellis and filled the space with a low sofa and Middle Eastern style poufs to sit on. It reminded Lucy of an Arabian souk or bazaar with the bright colors—fuchsia, teal, saffron, lime, and bright orange—on everything from cushions to pillows and piles of blankets in baskets. Palm plants and hanging baskets of flowers filled every corner. Someone had set a table—Hattie, she assumed—with a gorgeous vintage Kantha quilt from India covered in a botanical design. Seated around the table were Mark, Sam, and Gracie.

Lucy laughed. Of course, Hattie would have gathered them up one by one and deposited her group of special favorites at the only table left on the property, even though it was her private space and not part of the café. Mark patted a spot between himself and Gracie for her to sit. Lucy gave Sam a squeeze on the shoulder before settling in. There was room for one more at the head of the table, but seeing the size of the crowd outside, she wondered if Hattie would be able to make an appearance or if she'd be run off her feet helping serve customers.

She didn't have to wait long—Kai opened the french doors connected to Hattie's living room and proceeded to help Hattie roll out a triple-decker cart. Coffee and tea trays were on the top shelf. Kai moved them over to a side table for serving. Platters covered the other two shelves. Sam jumped up and helped Hattie place them all on the table so Kai could run back to his waiting tables.

Mark whistled. "Lucy, I know we were supposed to have a nice, quiet breakfast date, but I think this might be a better option." He winked at her, knowing she was already drooling over several of the dishes Hattie unwrapped in front of them.

"Hattie," Mark continued, "this is amazing. Are you sure you can spare the time? It seems nuts out there!"

"A girl's gotta eat." She waved to the generous feast covering the table. "And the sooner, the better."

Lucy didn't need to be told twice. Not when there were biscuits and gravy at stake!

Chapter Seventeen

Sand emptied out of Lucy's sandal as she shook it off. Balanced on one foot, she wiped the sole of the other before slipping her sandal back on and climbing the wooden stairs to the upper level of the boardwalk.

Mark held her bag, which was now stuffed full of smaller bags from the various booths where she'd shopped. The number and quality of the artisans this year had caught her by surprise, as did the variety and beauty of the things on offer. She'd bought far more than she intended, including jewelry for herself and gifts for family and friends, but also clever crafts and artwork that she couldn't pass by.

Her favorite had to be the sea glass sun catcher that mirrored the stained-glass window in the church tower. It cost more than she liked to spend, but the hours of painstaking work put into the piece more than justified the price. She could imagine hanging it in her home and never growing tired of it.

Mark had slipped off a few times, leaving her to shop alone, but he'd always returned within a few minutes. She suspected he was doing a little early Christmas shopping too. After the large brunch they'd consumed at Hattie's, neither of them wanted lunch, but now that the afternoon was getting later, many of the food offerings on the boardwalk began to smell good to them both.

Mark bought a fried chocolate-covered cookie, but Lucy turned down a taste, holding out for the caramel apples she knew were just down the way. She'd had them as a child—crisp, sweet apples covered in warm, gooey caramel and then dipped in fun toppings like nuts, sprinkles, or mini chocolate chips and drizzled over with any sauce she wanted. Drooling, she went ahead to get in line. Mark promised to finish his cookie, then come find her.

As she stood in line, she checked her messages. No texts, but she'd missed several calls and had new a voicemail. She hated voicemail. Why couldn't people just be reasonable and text? She looked at her missed calls. Several from her grandmother, one from Captain Andy Harrison, and one from Gracie. She looked up to see she was next in line, so she decided to order her candy apple before checking her voicemails. *I'll miss out altogether if I don't get it now.*

She chose a white chocolate caramel apple with white chocolate chips and pumpkin spice drizzle. The girl working at the stand had just handed over her cellophane-wrapped treat when a voice spoke into her ear. She jumped and turned, expecting to see that it was Mark who'd startled her. She found herself staring into the same sea-glass green eyes as Mark, but they were in Captain Harrison's unsmiling face.

"What did you say?" Lucy asked. The boardwalk was not a quiet place, between the crowds, the live music playing on the beach stage, and the carnival-style sounds coming from the rides and attractions.

"I need you to come down to the station," he repeated.

"Oh, sure, I'll have Mark bring me by before dinner." She smiled at him. "He's around here somewhere. You're welcome to join us."

The corners of Captain Harrison's mouth turned up before he pressed his lips together. "Sorry, Lucy, I can't do that. I need you to come to the station with me now." He looked around to see if Mark was close by—both stood a head taller than most of the crowd—but failed to spot him. "We'll text Mark from the car and let him know where you are."

A wave of anxiety hit Lucy. "Did something happen to my grandfather? I just saw my grandmother's been calling. I was going to call her back. Just tell me. What's wrong?"

"No, it's nothing like that. As far as I know, everyone is fine." His face had softened a little at the panic in her voice, but then he added, "I need you to answer some questions. Down at the station. Please, come with me." He held out his arm to indicate the direction.

Confused, Lucy followed him away from the beach and boardwalk and toward the parking lot. Once they were away from the noise, she asked, "Am I being detained?"

He turned and looked at her over his sunglasses. "I don't want to detain you. I'd rather you came willingly."

He'd parked his police cruiser in a reserved spot near the front of the parking lot. When he walked around to the back door of the passenger seat and opened it, motioning for her to get in, she knew she was in trouble.

From the back seat, she texted Mark to let him know what happened and then put out an SOS to Sam—who was still her lawyer—and her grandparents. She even texted Hattie. She didn't know what was coming, but she wanted all the backup she could get.

Lucy couldn't believe it. She found herself sitting across from Captain Andy Harrison at the same smudged table in the same dingy room she'd endured before. The now-retired Officer Mooney had picked her to be his number one suspect for everything—the theft of a sailing ship, the assault of an elderly woman in her store, the disappearance of her grandparents, and even her own kidnapping. One thing was different then, though. Andy Harrison had believed in her innocence.

"I can't be seen playing favorites, Lucy. I hope you understand. I have to record this interview, and the charges are serious. Unless you have an alibi or some other means of answering that clears you, I will have to do what the law requires." Captain Harrison sounded sympathetic, but the look on his face was grim.

"I don't know how you could believe her over me. You know me!" Lucy was adamant. She was also angry—boiling, steaming, hopping mad. She knew she needed to keep her cool, though.

"I have to take the complaint seriously. She wants to press charges and swore on oath that you attacked her." The police captain rubbed the back of his neck. "So, tell me again. Why did you invite Camilla Delacruz to the bookstore?"

"I didn't invite her. I wouldn't invite her. That's all I'm saying until Sam gets here. In other words, I want my lawyer." Lucy had watched far too many courtroom dramas to not insist on having her lawyer present during any questioning.

"If you didn't do anything wrong, you don't have anything to worry about." Andy Harrison leaned in and made sure she was looking him in the eyes. "Lawyering up makes you look guilty."

"Don't even try that line with me. I know better. You know I like you a great deal, as a person and as my boyfriend's father, but right now, you're not on my side. I understand that it's your job—and you're good at it—but I know how easy it is for things to get twisted and the wrong people to get into trouble. So, lawyer, please. No more questions."

"Fine. But I'm not your enemy here." He stood up and

crossed to the door, opening it just a crack to speak to someone on the other side.

No, Cami is my enemy here. She pinched the bridge of her nose, willing away the headache brewing behind her eyes. It was all she could do not to cry. At the station, she'd had to surrender her phone and wallet, and even worse, her caramel apple. If anything happened to her apple, she'd make Cami pay.

He continued to confer in hushed tones with the officer outside the door until a commotion arose somewhere down the hall. Several loud voices carried on an argument. Then she heard a crash, and Captain Harrison ran out of the room, leaving her alone. The door was weighted and shut behind him, but not before Lucy heard more yelling.

Good, she thought. *Help is here.*

Thirty minutes later, she sat on a cold metal bench inside a disgusting cell. The senior lady next to her wouldn't shut up, and Lucy had enough of her already. She yelled for the guard, who seemed to ignore her. "Can someone please get me out of here? At least give me a private cell!"

Sam and Captain Harrison came through a secured door and approached Lucy, who now had her hands wrapped around the steel bars. She wondered why they hadn't put her in a more modern holding cell, but having an angry, off-her-rocker roommate was the last straw.

"You're just in time," she said to Sam. "Can you please get me out of here? Before I do something I regret?"

"Sorry, Lucy, I can't get you out just yet. We'll have to finish the interview with Captain Harrison before he decides whether to charge you or let you go home." He nodded his head toward her cell mate. "I can do something about that, though. They're going to release her if she pays her fine."

"I'm not paying any fine!" her cellmate yelled.

Andy Harrison just rolled his eyes and leaned against the wall.

"I'll pay the fine for her, Sam, just write a check for me and I'll reimburse it immediately. I'm gonna go nuts if I have to spend one more minute locked up in here with her."

The woman regarded Lucy with cold eyes and said, "Is that any way to talk about your grandmother? I came here to bust you out!"

"And how is that working out for you?" Lucy was at her limit. She knew her grandmother meant well, but Glo could be a little too feisty for her own—or anyone else's—good. "When the desk sergeant refused to bring me out or let you in, you threw her bell *at her head*. In a police station, in front of three other policemen. What did you think was going to happen?"

"I didn't throw it at her head," she said. "I threw it at the wall. If I'd wanted to hit her, I would have! She was being a total cow to me."

"Telling you no is not the same as someone being a cow. You need to apologize to her, pay the fine, and let Sam take you home. I mean, for heaven's sake, she's almost as old as you are and sits two rows behind you in church!"

Her grandmother's shoulders slumped. "You're right. I don't know what came over me. All I could think about was you being held here against your will, and I just lost it." She looked over at Captain Harrison and said, "I *am* sorry. If you let me out, I'll go pay the fine and apologize to Marjory. But you have to understand that Lucy didn't do anything wrong. I won't let you railroad my only granddaughter."

Captain Harrison stood up straight and said, "Ma'am, I know you didn't mean to do that. I recognize PTSD when I see it. We're not holding Lucy captive, I promise. And I have no plans to railroad anybody." He pulled the keys from his pocket and opened the door. "Now be on your best behavior and go straight home. Let Mark drive you because heaven knows you should not be behind the wheel of a car right now. Sam can stay with Lucy, okay?"

Her grandmother nodded. Lucy had never seen her quite so subdued. She put her arms around her grandmother for a hug and whispered in her ear. "Thank you for coming for me, Grandma. If they don't let me out by dinner, bake me a cake with a stick of dynamite in it." She wanted to see her grandmother smile and was rewarded with a beaming grin.

"You better believe I will!" She kissed Lucy on the cheek and followed Captain Harrison out of the cell and through the door.

Andy hadn't bothered closing the cell where Lucy remained behind with Sam. She wasn't sure why, so she quizzed Sam. "Am I supposed to break out of jail now?"

Sam laughed. "No, you're not under arrest. He just put you back here with Glo so she'd calm down. She was threatening to burn the whole place down if she didn't see her granddaughter immediately. These cells aren't used anymore. In fact, they don't even lock. He was just pretending to unlock the door." Sam shook his head at her and added, "He wanted to teach her a lesson.

"Come with me. We'll meet him in the conference room for questions, and then I'll have you out of here. Just look at me before you answer anything. If I nod, go ahead and answer truthfully. If I shake my head, just refuse to answer even if you think the answer will help you. Just trust me and follow my lead."

Lucy tried to wrap her head around the events of the last half hour as she followed Sam to the much nicer conference room. It was clean and had cushioned seats, even. It was the Ritz compared to the grubby interview room she'd been in before.

"Cami told Dr. Wilson and an officer that you invited her to come to the bookstore, claiming you had information on the person who killed her father. She says that you then took her downstairs into the basement, and you hit her in the head. She says the last thing she remembers is you standing over her, injecting her with something in a syringe. Tell me now if *any* of that is true. We have privacy in this room, so you can speak freely." Sam patted her shoulder.

Lucy couldn't believe the nerve of that woman. She wasn't even who she claimed to be, and now she was making wild accusations. "None of that is true, Sam. But you need to know, I did find her in the basement unconscious and called for help. You know I'd never hurt anyone. Dr. Wilson came, and he and my grandparents decided to bring her upstairs and put her outside. Mark carried her. It just seemed safer after all that happened this summer." She filled him in on the research she'd done that led her to believe Cami and her father were not who they claimed to be, as well.

Sam nodded. "I wish someone would have called me when it happened, but thank you for telling me the truth now. I really liked Cami, but I realized something was off with her the day your friend Gracie fell into the tunnel. We'll save this conversation for later, but in the meantime, I just want to say I'm sorry for not seeing it sooner. Now let's get this interview over with."

Chapter Eighteen

The aggravations kept coming. Mark was late picking her up, and she hadn't eaten since the granola bar Sam slipped her the day before. The interview took a long time, or so it seemed to Lucy, and many of the questions were repeated. When Andy Harrison said he had to do things by the book and give her no special treatment, he wasn't kidding. In fact, Lucy was pretty sure he had gone too far in the other direction. Sam had objected several times, stating that the question had been asked and answered already.

When the police captain raised his voice to her, Sam had finally put a stop to it by asking if Lucy was being charged or if they were free to go. However, as they walked out, she was told not to leave town and to make herself available for further questioning as the investigation continued. She was beyond upset and shaken when Sam brought her out into the waiting room at the station and asked for her belongings. But when the clerk informed Lucy that her caramel apple had to be thrown away, she lost it. It was just one insult too many.

Mark was pacing outside when Sam and Lucy exited. He'd been made to wait in the parking lot for causing a disturbance. Everyone was aware now that he was Captain Harrison's son, which was likely the reason he hadn't been put in a cell with Lucy's grandmother to calm her down.

Sam had walked over to the station, so Mark drove them both back to Lucy's home, where they discussed the events of the last few days. Sam went over some instructions with each of them in case they were brought in for separate questioning. Lucy's stomach hurt from the anger and stress, so she went straight to bed without eating. Mark kissed her on the forehead and promised to pick her up the following morning at ten with breakfast to go.

Lucy zipped her jacket and walked farther down the drive. It was already ten-thirty, and no sign of Mark yet. She didn't want to wait inside because she felt restless, and her patience with her grandparents was at an all-time low. She was both hurt and angry, thinking they still didn't trust her even though they'd said otherwise and claimed they'd include her in everything from now on.

She walked a little way down the sidewalk toward the community garden that occupied the edge of her grandparents' property. They donated the space many years ago, and it had proved popular. There were plots for growing produce and flowers but also a park-like place for tourists and townspeople alike to sit and enjoy the old-growth redwoods and the colorful ornamental landscaping.

Lucy sat down on one of the cast iron benches that circled a massive oak tree and called Mark. His phone went straight to voicemail, so Lucy leaned her back against the tree and closed her eyes. If he didn't show soon, she would walk to Hattie's and look for him there, where she could eat a breakfast burrito the size of her head.

She opened one eye when a passing vehicle tapped its horn. Mark went up to her driveway and turned around. He pulled up onto the verge near her and leaned across the cab of his truck to open her door.

"I'm so sorry I'm late! You must be starving. Ready to go?" Mark gave her his winningest smile. "I have a surprise for you."

Her heart skipped a beat as she studied his face, looking for any clue about what the surprise might be. For half a second, she imagined a ring in a box with Mark on bended knee. *What is wrong with me? A killer on the loose and a crazy woman trying to get me locked up, and that's where my brain goes?* Oy. She had to laugh it off as she jumped into the truck and settled in. "You're right. I am starving. You could say I'm delirious with hunger, even."

"Well, I'm glad to hear it. Hang on for five more minutes, and then we'll feast like kings!" Mark did another U-turn and headed out. He turned off the highway onto a gravel road, then turned again onto a dirt track surrounded by dense brush that gave way to a thick stand of evergreen trees that dimmed the sun. Lush ferns grew on the side of the road at the base of the trees. It felt like the forest primeval.

She'd never been this way and had no idea where they were headed, but just when Lucy's eyes had adjusted to the lower level of light, the pickup rounded a corner into bright, dazzling sunlight. She shielded her eyes as Mark pulled off the road and into a meadow.

"What is this place?" she asked. The wide field crowned the high point of a gently sloping hill. A little way down from where they parked, a pond sparkled. Beyond that, the ground rolled away in undulating curves rimmed by several acres of beautiful redwood trees. Lucy gasped in delight as a bottle-blue dragonfly swooped by her head and then came back around for a landing on her forearm.

"It's our picnic spot. I hope you like it." Mark pulled a cooler from the back of the truck, followed by a blanket, two camp chairs, and a folding table. Lucy removed the chairs from their carrying bags and opened them while Mark set up the table on one of the picnic blankets he'd laid out on the ground. After one more trip to the truck, he returned with a thermos and a plain brown paper bag, which he stashed behind his chair.

Lucy was already elbow-deep in the cooler, pulling out plates of cut fruit, scones, and cheese danish, rolls of prosciutto and cubes of white cheddar, hard-boiled eggs, yogurt cups, chocolate chip muffins, and granola.

Mark poured two cups of steaming hot chocolate into paper cups and sat down, letting Lucy make a plate for herself before getting one of his own. Lucy noticed and appreciated the gallantry, but she was self-aware enough to realize he might have just been worried about getting between her and the cold cuts of Canadian bacon.

She was glad Mark didn't have much to say while she polished off everything on her plate. There was only time for chewing, not answering questions. He seemed to sense that she wasn't quite full yet—he opened the pack of granola and shook some into a yogurt cup for her.

Lucy swirled the crunchy topping into the creamy yogurt and made appreciative noises in his direction. She was dating the perfect man. Other boyfriends she'd had, especially in college, would eat their entire meal and still want half of hers!

At last, the primal hunger passed, so she slowed down, sipping the hot chocolate from her cup. Mark looked as if he was trying to hide an amused smile behind his own cup.

"Tell Hattie I said thanks for breakfast. It was delicious, and it was the best thing I've eaten since she fed us breakfast yesterday!" Lucy rubbed her stomach in a circular motion.

"Hey, I made this, not Hattie. Well, I bought the baked goods from Honey, but I made all the rest myself."

"You did? I can't believe you went to all this trouble for me. That's incredibly sweet, Mark."

"It wasn't any trouble. Hattie taught me everything I know, so it didn't take long to put things together. However," he said, "I will take credit for this." He reached around behind his chair and grabbed the paper bag. "Close your eyes."

Lucy laughed but closed her eyes. She shook off the image of a ring in a box again, knowing that whatever it was, it wasn't that. She believed it would be something good, though!

Something crinkled, and then Mark said, "Okay, open your eyes."

When she looked up, Mark stood beside her chair, holding a beautiful, cellophane-wrapped caramel apple with white chocolate, pumpkin sauce, and white chocolate chips. She jumped from her chair and wrapped her arms around him, kissing his face a dozen times. *My goodness, he really is the perfect man.*

"There was a long line already when I got there, and they weren't even open yet. Getting this apple is what made me late picking you up." Mark gave her ponytail a playful yank. "I'm really sorry about what happened yesterday."

"I can't believe you went and stood in line for me like that. I was so disappointed about losing that apple! Of course, I will share it with you." Lucy put the apple back in the paper bag and handed it to Mark. "Let's put that in the cooler with the rest of the cold food for now. I'm stuffed! And you have no reason to be sorry about what happened. You didn't cause that."

Mark pressed his lips together. "But I wasn't with you. If I had been, I might have been able to talk Andy out of taking you to the station. I feel awful about how you were treated, and Sam does too."

"I don't think you could have talked him out of it. He has a job to do, and he's in the public eye. I'm sure he just treated me the way they'd treat any other suspect. It wasn't fun, though, and it may take me a while to look at him the same way, but I don't want it to affect your relationship with him. You've only known he was your father for a few months—you're still getting to know each other, so don't be upset with him, okay?"

"Lucy, I can't help that. I care about you, and I want to protect you. I was beside myself when you were being questioned. I can't understand why he would believe Cami's story at all, especially since he knows you so well. He must know you'd never do the things she's accused you of." Mark pulled her a little closer and wrapped her in his strong arms. "I'm going to talk to him, set him straight about all this."

"No, Mark, don't do that. On some level, I don't think he does believe Cami, and I don't want you to talk to him. Let Sam handle it. It's what we pay him for, and he's doing a good job. I'm sure this will all be cleared up, and we can put it behind us."

"I know Cami isn't a good person, and she isn't who she claims to be—she's no pastor's daughter—but I still can't understand why she was in your root cellar. How could she know what's down there? I didn't think anyone else knew, so how did she get there? And who really knocked her out?"

"I don't know. I really wish I did. Someone obviously knows more about this town and its history than we thought. I didn't know about the tunnel that connected under the church or the hidden chamber under the trading post. There's a lot more going on than I think we've been told, and I think my grandparents know a lot more than they've let on."

She filled Mark in on the conversation she'd overheard her grandparents having about the cameras being down and their lack of trust and about the stacks of obstacles that were now hiding the four doors in the basement. A lump came up in her throat as she explained how hard it was, knowing they didn't want her involved and that they didn't have faith in her to keep the family's secrets.

Mark held her, letting the sadness run its course. After a time, though, she felt other emotions looming, namely anger and fear.

"It's not just that they should trust me because I'm their granddaughter. I'm terrified that if they don't trust me, something terrible will happen. Their silence and secret-keeping nearly cost them their lives once already. It put the rest of us in grave danger too. And now I'm afraid it's going that way again. I can't let that happen. It's up to me to keep them safe."

Mark sighed. "And it's up to me to keep you safe. If you're planning something, I'm in. I don't want you going it alone."

Lucy started to deny it, but a plan was rolling around in her mind already, and there was no way she could make it work alone. In fact, she might need all the help she could get.

"Deal," she said.

"That was too easy. You're not just telling me that so you can go off on your own and do what you want anyway, are you?" His raised eyebrows hinted that he wasn't serious.

"I mean it. If I'm right, we might be able to keep everyone safe, figure out who killed the faux-pastor, and teach Cami a lesson all the same time. But we're going to need reinforcements."

She outlined her idea to Mark, who peppered her with a few questions. But in the end, he was on board.

"Since this will take a day or two to put in place, how about we stick with my plan for today?" Mark winked at Lucy and waggled his eyebrows at her in what she thought was an effort to be enticing. She tried to repress a giggle but failed.

"What did you have in mind?" she asked. She gave an exaggerated wink back.

"I thought we'd take a romantic stroll around the pond, where there are about a hundred dragonflies buzzing around. But maybe I'll just toss you in the pond instead!"

His wide smile didn't make Lucy think he was kidding about that, so she yelped and ran away from him, laughing all the while. Mark growled at her and gave pursuit, catching her quickly. He picked her up and tossed her over his shoulder, which made her laugh even harder. Instead of carrying her to the pond, however, he rolled her off his shoulder and onto the picnic blanket, where he kissed her until she stopped laughing and kissed him back.

Chapter Nineteen

Lucy sat by the pond on a log Mark had folded a blanket over. The afternoon sun was framed by the descending valley that led all the way to the Pacific, whose blue horizon she could barely see from her vantage point. Mark had been full of surprises all day. He'd taken her on that romantic walk through the trees and around the pond, showing her several beauty spots along the way.

Her favorite was the waterfall that tumbled down the side of a hill through green ferns and all sorts of leafy vegetation to feed a pretty, shallow stream that bubbled and sang over a rocky bottom. A weather-beaten wooden footbridge crossed over the water to the trail that continued down the hillside. They'd stopped on the bridge and took pictures in every direction, and Mark even agreed to pose for a picture with Lucy. He wasn't much for selfies, but he was happy to take the picture with her.

They'd wandered back up the other side of the hill—it was a bit steeper and not as easy to navigate, but Mark always helped her over the difficult spots, and she found herself enjoying the exertion. After the hike, though, she wanted to rest awhile, so she lay down on the blanket, her head resting on Mark's thigh as she watched the clouds race across the sky.

Lucy must have fallen asleep at some point because she woke

up alone with Mark's jacket draped over her. She rubbed her eyes and sat up, expecting to see Mark nearby, but he wasn't anywhere in sight. She stood up and felt the beginnings of tomorrow's soreness as she stretched. Then she headed up to the truck, figuring he'd gone to get some drinks from the cooler or an extra blanket. But he wasn't there either.

With no messages on her phone, she texted him and waited to hear back. Finally, she wandered down to the pond, where she found the blanket folded on the log and two other logs upturned next to it. He'd brought down a couple of water bottles and her caramel apple for them to share and placed them on the bigger of the two logs for a table.

Where are you? She knew he had to be around somewhere. It had only been ten minutes or so that she'd been awake and looking for him, but it felt longer. She knew he'd be back—unless something had happened to him. What if he'd gone into the woods for something and gotten hurt? She pushed the feeling of foreboding away. If anyone was capable in the woods, it was Mark.

In the meantime, she enjoyed watching the dragonflies as they dipped and dove, competing for meals and mates. The sun lit their wings and bodies at a low angle, making them appear at times as if they were flying jewels with diamond wings. They were stunning, and Mark wasn't exaggerating when he said there were at least a hundred of them around the pond.

She'd just about decided to go looking for Mark when he came out of the tree line near the edge of the pond.

"Oh, good. You're awake!" He beckoned for her to join him. "I made a, uh, comfort station for you."

"A what?"

She couldn't imagine what he meant. Nothing in the woods brought the word *comfort* to mind. She took his hand and followed him a short distance into a thicket of young trees. He'd set up a tall, gray pop-up tent behind an area of thick brush.

"Come see." He led her over and unzipped the door. Inside he'd placed a camp toilet, complete with an attached roll and a shelf with hand sanitizer and biodegradable wipes. She could see he was proud of his efforts, so she stuffed the feeling of embarrassment and tried her best to look impressed.

"That's amazing! I didn't know they made things like this!" Lucy ventured closer to the tent, and Mark pushed a button on a small light hanging inside the makeshift loo.

"It's completely safe and hygienic too. You just do what one normally does, and it goes into a composting bag, which bag drops into the hole I've dug beneath. So, when you close the lid, it automatically seals it up and sends it down. Later, when I take it down, it's just a matter of replacing the dirt to fill the hole."

Lucy felt a little bit horrified, but it *was* impressive. And now that he mentioned it, her bladder had woken up and decided that the current arrangement was both acceptable and urgently required.

"Okay, perfect. Thank you." She pushed him away from the opening and stepped inside. "Could you, um, go away?"

The look of surprise on his face was replaced with understanding, so he zipped the door closed for her and made a hasty retreat. She eyed the low-sitting contraption, feeling uncertain about it, but she knew she no longer had a choice. Thankfully, it was much better than her childhood memories, where going in the woods was a much more primitive experience.

She was touched. Mark really had tried to think of everything. As she returned to the pond, she wondered what else he had in store. She didn't have to wait long to find out. He'd already cut the apple in half and put each half on a little plate, but there was something on the table that hadn't been there before. It was a little gift bag with blue paper peeking from the top, and it was just about the right size to hold a jewelry box.

"Thank you for doing that," she said. "I felt a little bougie in that five-star facility, but it was such a nice surprise. Are you sure it's okay to dig a latrine out here?"

"Don't worry about that. The owner's fine with it. Besides, no one will ever know but us!"

Lucy sat down, eyeing the caramel apple. It had been some time since their brunch, and that apple wasn't going to eat itself. She ignored the gift bag on the table and picked up her half. Mark had cut it so the wooden skewer remained with her half, and he'd jabbed his half with a pocketknife to hold it.

"Cheers!" Lucy tapped her apple to Mark's.

"*Buon appetito!*" he replied, followed by a groan of delight as he bit into the rich confection.

It didn't take them long to polish off the treat. Lucy tried not to stare at the gift bag on the table, but her mind whirled, trying to figure out what might be in there. She didn't want to be rude, but the anticipation was killing her. She studiously avoided looking at the table for at least thirty seconds, but when her eyes landed on Mark's face, she could see he was enjoying watching her squirm.

"Would you like to open your present now?" he asked.

"For me?" She pretended to bat her eyelashes.

"No, it's for Sam. Of course, it's for you! Open it. I can't wait to see what you think."

She thought it couldn't be an engagement ring even though that thought had popped up twice. He'd be on one bended knee for that, never mind their sticky fingers from the caramel apple.

She reached into the bag and pulled out a long jewelry box and a square of cardstock with something printed on it. It read, "Seaview Annual Sea Glass Festival – Grand Prize – Amateur

Artisan." She turned it over, but there wasn't anything written on the back. She raised her eyebrows, trying to puzzle it out.

"Just open the box, Luce."

She opened the box and gasped. "Oh, Mark, it's beautiful!"

She pulled the bracelet from its mount and held it up in the light of the soon-setting sun. It was made of many tiny, silver loops woven with strands of silver wire wrapped around pieces of colorful, polished sea glass. She'd never seen anything like it. It was a substantial piece but still delicate and feminine.

She wrapped it around her wrist, securing it with a silver toggle in the shape of a heart, then twisted it around to examine each section in turn. "I don't know what to say! You bought this for me? I can see why it won the grand prize." She pressed her hand to her heart, willing herself not to cry. "Thank you. It's perfect."

"I'm so glad you like it, Luce. I didn't buy it, though. I made it! See, all the pieces of sea glass are the ones we picked up on our beach date. I could tell you wanted them, but you let me have them when I asked. One of my recruits used to help his mother make jewelry, and he taught me how to do wire wrapping and make a bracelet."

She let out a low whistle. "I'm so impressed! I can't believe you made this for me! And you entered it in the art show. That's amazing."

"I would have given it to you earlier, but our date was interrupted." A look of anger flashed across his features. "I still can't believe that happened. If Andy hadn't taken you in for questioning . . ." He closed his eyes and sighed.

"I know he was just doing his job, Mark. I'm not mad, and I don't want you to be either. I'm sorry it ruined our date—especially since I would've loved to see you win a prize at the festival—but honestly, I couldn't be happier. This has been a perfect day, and you gave me the perfect present, and I get to have you all to myself. It means the world to me."

She stood up and leaned over to kiss him, but he had other ideas. He grabbed her around the waist and spun her around, sitting her on his lap. She was surprised by the sudden move, but then he pointed down the valley leading to the ocean. The sun slipped just below the horizon. Amber and gold clouds painted the higher elevations, fading to burnished bronze nearer the water.

For a moment, the sun's light reflected back up into the sky, making it look almost like an hourglass. Then she caught the rare green flash that sometimes happens when the conditions are perfect.

"Did you see that?" She turned to look at Mark. "Tell me you saw that!"

"I did! I've seen it a few times, mostly out at sea. Pirates used to say that the green flash meant someone was leaving the world of the dead and coming back to this world." He hugged her closer to his chest. "There are lots of myths and superstitions about it, but the science behind it is even cooler."

Lucy snuggled deeper into his arms. "Science, myth, whatever. Let's just call it what it is—it's *pretty*. Just so unbelievably pretty!"

Chapter Twenty

Monday morning chaos was in full swing when Lucy slipped down the back stairs and opened a can of cat food for Tor. She needed him to be well-fed and not chase her around, meowing for his next meal. She refilled his water and his dry food, too, and put down a handful of cat treats just to be safe. He looked up at her as if to question her life choices but then decided it wasn't any of his business as long as cat treats were involved.

An energetic story time was in progress in the bookstore. Usually, Lucy would have been present for it, but today her grandfather was in charge of reading to the three excited pre-school classes who came in once a month as a special treat. Many of the parents came as chaperones for the field trip—not so much to help as to take cute pictures of their kids—so the front had standing room only.

Outside, a crew had set up scaffolding on one side of the Victorian that reached all the way to the third floor. The exterior painting had all been finished previously, but a portion of the trim waited for Gracie to recover enough to complete it. Lucy had popped her head out of her window earlier that morning to say hello and was pleased to learn that her friend was planning to be there all day, working on the front of the house first, then moving to the back to paint from both a ladder and from a perch on the second-floor roof. That fit into Lucy's plans perfectly—the more distractions, the better.

Currently, Glo was escorting Allen Morgan, the alarm system specialist, around the perimeter of the yard, instructing him on where she wanted additional video surveillance. He'd originally put a home security system in for Lucy when she was living in the house alone—her grandparents missing and presumed deceased. He hadn't let Lucy pay then, citing his gratitude for the help her grandfather had given him with history homework and kindling a love for history in him as a teen. He'd also refused payment on the grounds that he didn't want to get in trouble with Dr. Wilson, his wife's foster father, who felt it his duty to look after Lucy.

Lucy imagined he'd let her grandmother pay now, considering she was asking for a major upgrade in security systems, with motion lights and cameras outside and more cameras in the bookstore and various areas around the main floor of the house.

Her grandmother had been only too happy to have him stop by when Lucy suggested it was time for the routine maintenance for the alarm system he'd put in place, and she seemed very agreeable to the suggestion that it was time to add a layer of protection for their home and business. What she didn't know was that Lucy planned to use the cover of having the security system turned off to do a little breaking and entering of her own.

She peered out the kitchen window, then stepped out into the backyard. She checked to see that her grandmother was still in the front, and no one was approaching from either side of the house. Then she texted Mark the all-clear. A few seconds later, Mark, followed closely by Sam, emerged from the tree line at the back of the property. Both men zipped across the yard and into the door Lucy held open.

Silently, the three of them made their way into the basement, with Lucy bringing up the rear and closing the door behind them. They'd agreed to go first to the root cellar and see if there was anything they'd missed when Lucy found Cami unconscious behind the bookcase. Lucy was sure her grandparents had put the room back in order, but there was still a chance of finding some clue that had been overlooked.

She lifted the inset door leading to the root cellar and then followed Mark and Sam down. When it was shut overhead, she pulled the light switch and joined them on the bare floor. She breathed a sigh of relief that they could talk now and not risk being overheard.

Sam looked anxious—he hadn't been exactly eager to sign on to Lucy's plan, preferring to let the police handle the investigation. He also pointed out that her grandparents were his employers, and he wasn't sure sneaking around behind their backs was the right move. Only when Lucy pointed out the protective nature of what she wanted to do, did he finally acquiesce.

If they could figure out what Cami was doing here and who knocked her out, they could clear Lucy of suspicion. They also hoped to find out what the pretend pastor was doing that got him killed in the tunnel below the church crypt. But to do any of that, Lucy felt sure she needed to know what her grandparents were still hiding from her. Without that knowledge, she'd never be able to put all the puzzle pieces together, and she needed the whole picture to keep them safe.

The trio knew that one of the walls in the root cellar opened to reveal a staircase that led up into the house and down into a lower level of caverns. Lucy had yet to explore the area below because her grandparents had pretty much forbidden it upon their return, citing dangerous and crumbling tunnels. She wasn't sure they were telling her the truth now, though, and added it to the list of things to check into as soon as possible.

Mark easily swung the shelves away from the wall and pointed out to Sam where Lucy had found Cami. The wall behind the shelves was solid rock but had strange circular indentations on the face of it. Lucy reminded them that it was also the place she'd found a scrap of paper with the single word "illuminate" on it and that she once thought she'd heard something moving behind the wall but could never find a way to open it.

They searched the floor and the shelves but found nothing to indicate that Cami or her attacker had ever been there. With nothing further to be gained, they climbed the root cellar stairs and peeped into the basement. When she was satisfied they were alone, she led the men out and gently lowered the door to resettle in the wooden floor.

Sam and Mark quietly moved the stack of boxes a few feet in front of the door they blocked. They'd chosen the door closest to the root cellar as their first target and hoped that the keys Lucy swiped would work. Each door faced one of the four cardinal directions, and Mark, with his Coast Guard training, knew intuitively that the door in front of them faced north and should correspond to the key marked *Borealis*.

Lucy had discovered the keys in a hidden compartment in her grandmother's desk over the summer. Each one had a tag written in Latin that stood for a direction, and she believed they belonged to the basement doors. Those rooms were off limits to her for her entire childhood and no amount of begging had ever granted her access. Her stomach did flip-flops as she handed the key to Sam to try in the lock.

The key fit, and a series of clicks followed after Sam turned it. A cold rush of air caused Lucy to shiver as the door opened. Mark went in first and located a light switch. When he turned it on, Lucy was surprised to see books on shelves lining the walls and in glass display cases throughout the room. There was also what looked like a workstation in the back corner with an array of tools and materials.

Lucy pulled the door closed behind her, taking it all in. She noticed a screen on one wall with a set of digital numbers and pointed it out to Sam and Mark.

"It's a thermo-hygrometer," said Mark. We have them on the ship. It measures temperature and relative humidity.

Lucy nodded. "This is an archive room—everything in here is museum quality, I think!" She wandered over to the nearest shelf where several leather books were of a similar size were stored together. "These are all antique, maybe even first editions." She started to touch the spine of one but stopped herself. "Don't touch anything until we find some gloves. The oils in our hands could ruin these books."

Sam went over to one of the glass cases and peered at the book on display inside. "Lucy, look at this!"

"Oh wow, I can't believe it! If that's what I think it is . . ." Lucy circled the case, looking at the book on all sides. "It's an illuminated manuscript." The facing pages of the open book were covered in rich, colorful illustrations of a castle and farmland with workers and flocks surrounded by decorative borders of flowers and leaves.

Mark joined them at the display case and whistled. "I think it's gilded. Look. The edges look like they're coated with gold leaf."

Lucy bent over and tried to look at the cover from underneath. "I'm sure you're right. I've read about these, and once when I was a teenager, I got to see a couple of books like this in a traveling exhibit. But this one is far nicer than anything else I've ever seen."

Another display caught Lucy's eye. This one was inside a glass display case also, but it had a metal cage surrounding it. The book inside wasn't laid open like the others. Instead, the entire cover was gold filigree studded with colorful polished gemstones.

"Oh my," she breathed. "I know what this is." She could feel the goosebumps rising on her arms.

Mark and Sam hurried over to join her.

"Is that real? I mean, it has to be real. Look at the way it's locked up." Sam shook his head in disbelief.

"What exactly is it? It looks familiar somehow." Mark put an arm around Lucy as she shivered.

"It's a medieval treasure binding! I knew they were a thing, but I never thought I'd see one in person. It might look familiar because Disney made a model of one. In Sleeping Beauty, the movie opens with a book that's covered in jewels like this."

"How much is something like this worth?" Mark asked.

"I'm not sure you can put a number on something like this. It's priceless. It's a work of art, a piece of history . . . Usually something like this is in a private collection, and you'd never see it. A few museums have them on display, but not many have survived from the Middle Ages." Lucy chewed her bottom lip. How was it that her grandparents had such an incredible artifact, and she'd never known anything about it? Somehow it didn't seem right that it was locked away here instead of in a museum where the world could enjoy it.

Part of her wanted to run upstairs and confront her grandparents on the spot, but another part regretted what she'd learned. She looked around—the room was filled with books and even a few antiques. She'd known that the family had some hidden assets, but this was beyond what she imagined possible.

Her grandfather did have a collection of first edition and rare books in his own room upstairs, but nothing that a person couldn't get hold of from antique booksellers or even eBay. It made sense to keep a collection like this private, but she felt a hint of betrayal that it'd been kept even from her. Still, with the recent break-ins and her grandparents' abduction, she supposed it was best she hadn't known.

If this was what was stored in just one of the four rooms, she questioned whether she really did want to know what else was hidden. Each generation of her family had had to decide to keep the secret and continue to hide and protect what had fallen in their laps long ago. Her grandparents had decided to try to anonymously return a few items to where they belonged if it could be done without leaving a trail back to them, but something had gone sideways, and they came to the attention of exactly the wrong sort of people.

Lucy didn't like the idea of keeping such dangerous secrets going forward. The world had changed, and it would become harder and harder to hide certain things. Her stomach twisted, and she wondered what effect making these decisions would have had on her grandparents and her great-grandparents and even further up the line. She began to understand why her own parents took a different path that let them do good things in the world with some of the funds made available to them from the family's foundation while removing them from being directly involved. She was going to have to have a long talk with them one of these days when they were somewhere that didn't require a SAT phone or a ten-day boat journey just to have a conversation.

Lucy realized she was still staring at the beautiful book covered in gold and smooth gemstones. Mark stood beside her, watching her, concern evident on his face. She reached up an arm around his neck and welcomed the hug he gave her.

"This is a lot to take in, Lucy. Do you want to keep going or just call it a day? We don't have to do everything all at once."

She did feel overwhelmed. It was true. She was worried that

time was running out, though. The sooner they got to the bottom of things, the better.

"Let's keep looking. Where's Sam?" She glanced around the room but didn't see him.

"He found something—something I think you're going to want to check out." Mark untangled her arm from his neck but kept a hold of her hand. "Just over here. He found a door."

Mark led Lucy over to one of the walls that had several display cases and bookshelves arranged in front of it, as well as a storage cabinet tucked in one corner. He opened the cabinet door and motioned Lucy to go inside.

"Wait, does this lead to Narnia? Because I don't have my winter coat!" Lucy chuckled at her own joke. At least she could still crack herself up. That had to be a good sign, right?

Mark gave her a pressed smile. "While you were staring at the treasure binding book, Sam caught my eye and pointed to the interior of the cabinet and went inside. He popped his head out and waved for us to follow."

Lucy stepped into the cabinet and scooted over for Mark to join her. He looked around and figured out that the back panel slid across, revealing a door. Lucy closed the cabinet behind them while Mark went through first and held the door open for Lucy. The door opened on a landing with a stairwell—not unlike the one they'd found hidden behind the wall on the main floor of the house. However, this one only went down and not to the upper levels.

Lucy made her way carefully down the narrow stairs that curved around and ended on another landing below. Sam waited for them in front of what appeared to be a rock wall. The only thing in the entire landing area was a single bookshelf with several leather journals. These had to be the history journals her grandfather had spoken of, containing notes from each generation of the family who had lived in the home and safe-guarded the secrets kept there.

The feeling of déjà vu washed over Lucy. The staircase they'd found during the summer had a hidden mechanism that opened a door into the root cellar, where they discovered Lucy's grandfather. He'd been left in bad shape by the men who were determined to get their hands on the part of the treasure they believed must be there. She reached down a hand and found the identical piece and turned it. The door slid open to reveal the shelves that swung out in the root cellar where they'd begun their search. She couldn't believe it. There were two hidden passageways that led to that room.

She thought if over. If someone in the house needed to get to a hiding spot, they could go in through the hidden staircase in the niche wall on the main floor or access that same stairwell from upstairs and make their way down to the root cellar level. They could remain hidden behind the walls or go into the root cellar and out a different way.

There had to be a way to open the door from inside the root cellar, the one she was standing at now. But they hadn't discovered it yet. It made sense that someone might need to go into the treasure room and be able to leave through the root cellar too. One side led to a level lower than the cellar that accessed tunnels leading out and away from the property. Two had been sealed—the one to the derelict summer house and one that led from the wooded back of the property to a cliffside exit at a remote spot on the coast.

She was beginning to build a map in her mind of the warren of tunnels that ran under their property and through the town, even from the church crypts to the beach. It almost seemed as if the whole community was built on a foundation of secrets and intrigue and the misdeeds of the past. There was no doubt in her mind that her family had done their best to steward information and resources for the greater good, but she knew in her gut that even the best-kept secrets would one day be dragged into the light.

Lucy had Sam and Mark each grab some of the journals for her. By mutual agreement, they decided to leave the *borealis* compass room through the root cellar and climb back into the basement that way. It would be less difficult to explain, should they be discovered, than if they emerged from the locked compass room door itself. Sam swung the shelves away from the wall and waited until his companions were out. He pushed on the unit, and the rock wall slid back into place seamlessly. But they couldn't figure out how to open it again from the root cellar side.

Lucy packed the journals into a flour sack bag, and Sam carried them up the stairs. After lifting the door an inch and listening for a few moments to ensure no one was in the basement, the trio exited. Mark and Sam quietly pushed all the boxes they'd moved earlier back to their spot in front of the door.

Mark beckoned Lucy to the door on the west-facing wall. "Do you want to take a quick look inside? We spent more time than we planned in the first room, so we're maybe pushing it on the timing. It's up to you, though. We'll do whatever you want."

Sam looked at his phone. "I only have a few minutes. Andy has asked me to come down to the station for a chat."

"You should go ahead, then," Mark said. "We don't want to keep him waiting. If you can convince him that Lucy is innocent, that would be great." The two men shook hands, and Lucy walked Sam up to the door that led to the kitchen. No one was around, so she motioned him through, and he slipped out the back door.

By the time she returned to the basement, Mark had shifted the boxes out just enough to unlock the door, so Lucy tossed him the key ring. He selected the *Occidentalis*—or west—key and cracked the door. Lucy slipped through the opening but didn't find a light switch, so she turned on her phone's flashlight.

The room was empty. She was disappointed at first but then felt a wave of relief. She wasn't sure she was ready for another "cave of wonders" experience. She was about to back out when she noticed something sticking up from the floor. She went over for a closer look and realized it was a large vault door firmly encased in solid concrete. A wave of uneasiness washed over her. Something felt very wrong, but she couldn't pinpoint it. She backed out of the room and straight into Mark, who was waiting near the narrow wedge he'd opened for her to pass through. She stumbled, but he caught her around the waist and held her until she was steady on her feet.

"What is it, Lucy? You look like you've seen a ghost."

"Nothing. There's nothing there." She fumbled to lock the door. Something was there, buried in that safe, but it came with a heavy dose of dread in her mind. "Let's put this back and then save the rest for later. I want to curl up somewhere with the journals and see what I can learn from those. We'll try the other doors another day." *Maybe,* she thought. A shiver ran up her spine. *Maybe not.*

Chapter
Twenty-One

*L*ucy woke from troubled dreams before the sun was up and knew there was no going back to sleep. She didn't want to chance dreaming again. All night, it seemed she'd lived a dozen lives, facing danger and overcoming hardships while protecting secrets that could mean the difference between life and death if they were discovered.

She'd fallen asleep reading one of the smuggled journals and found it to be a mixture of history, household information, and notable incidents. The first portion of the book contained part of the story her grandfather had shared after his rescue. It covered the early days of the coastal region and the indigenous population, the Manilla treasure galleons that sailed up the west coast carrying Mexican gold and silver headed for Spain, and notes about the Spanish mission and the knight-priest who used the tunnels to hide relics and personal wealth. It also included a story about how the property became a rancho when Mexico overthrew the colonizing Spanish government.

It all gelled with what Lucy had learned from her grandfather, but there was one additional account in that journal that had upset her. The land where the house stood now and most of the area surrounding it had been gifted to a high-ranking Mexican soldier after the war. He built a large house for his wife and young daughter on the foundation of the former mission. While working in the cellar one day, he discovered the false wall built by the priest and tore it down, giving him access to the tunnels below. He made the mistake of telling his ranch hand about the discovery—a soldier who had retired from serving under him during the war.

The two planned to explore the tunnels together the next day, setting out with ropes and lanterns. When they found what the priest had hidden, the ranch hand killed his boss. He told the man's wife that her husband had died in an accident and fallen down and was lost. However, the daughter had followed the men into the tunnel and witnessed her father's murder.

She told her mother what had happened, so the woman hid her husband's gun in her skirt and pretended to believe the ranch hand's story. She asked him to take her to the place her husband died so she could say goodbye to him. The little girl's mother returned a few hours later, but the ranch hand never did.

Her mother sealed up the entrance to the tunnels, and they never spoke about it again. They lived there, running one of the only female *rancheros* in California history, along with the First Nations people she hired to help them run the place. They survived the Mexican–American War. Then came the gold rush.

Lucy knew the history from that point on: the first Patterson ancestor had escaped with his gold, his father, and his life by pretending their claim had failed and they were quitting and giving away their gear and equipment. They escaped by heading down along the coastal mountains instead of going toward San Francisco, where most of those who had a lucky strike tended to go. They lost their pursuers and ended up asking for shelter at the rancho.

The gold-panning son fell in love with the ranchero's daughter, and Lucy's family tree began in earnest. In the 1880s, they built one of the first Victorian houses on the West Coast, complete with hidden passageways and tunnel access that others explored and expanded. Someone did discover the bones of the two men, buried below in one of the tunnel offshoots and sealed up forever. Lucy guessed that one of the compass rooms led to their remains. The account went on to say that the earliest Patterson had recovered treasure from a destroyed ship hidden in the tunnels and had made "various and sundry other discoveries that left him filled with fear and wonder."

It was there that she'd fallen asleep. With her already fertile imagination and the other history she'd learned from her grandfather about the priest and his mission, it was no wonder that fantastic characters and adventures populated her dreams.

Lucy hid the journals under a stack of quilts in the antique armoire in her room and decided to get an early shower. She had a feeling it was going to be a long day.

Lucy sipped the spiced pumpkin apple cider, allowing the heat from the cup to warm her hands and her core. She'd been looking forward to Fall Festival for weeks. Seaview was always pretty in a picture postcard kind of way, but there was a special kind of beauty in autumn that was hard to beat. Everything seemed brighter and clearer—the blues of the sky and gemmy green waves coming to shore, the outline of the redwood trees in golden sunshine, the unhurried, shallow creeks and rivers wending their way down from the coastal mountains to the shore.

The town had outdone itself with charming décor, which meant there were tourists on every square inch of real estate trying to get the perfect selfie. People drove in from all over to witness the revealing of the greatest pumpkin of the year and shop for seasonal gifts, local wine, and lavender honey, and to lose themselves in corn and hay mazes. There were pumpkin patches on every other block, as well as a few along the highway leading to the coast. Children laughed and jumped in bouncy castles, rode tiny trains, fed animals in petting zoos, and chased each other through the rows of pumpkins.

She wandered along the row of vendors on Esperanza Street, stopping to chat with various business owners she'd come to know and checking out treats for sale. She couldn't resist a bag of pumpkin pie truffles coated in chocolate, which she hid in her purse after purchasing them. She knew better than to let Sam and Mark catch sight of them. Mark was working at the Coast Guard booth downtown, handing out mini pumpkins to children and talking to potential recruits about joining the service. His shift would be over soon, and she planned to meet up with him in time to see the weigh-in and award ceremony.

She passed by the kids' carving contest area, marveling at the creativity and skill on display. Each child who entered got to keep a pumpkin carving tool set and would be entered for prizes and drawings. It was pure pandemonium, and Lucy felt a tug of sympathy for the volunteers. There were at least a hundred pumpkins already on shelves waiting for judging, and no doubt, there would be twice as many before the day was done.

She was about to pass by the face-painting booth when someone called her name. She looked around but didn't see anyone, but then she felt a tug on her arm. It was Emma. She was a beaming jack-o'-lantern with orange face paint and a jagged, carved-out smile. Lucy dropped to one knee and gave her little friend a hug.

"Emma! I'm so happy to see you!" Lucy picked up one of Emma's braids and bopped her on the nose with the end of it.

"I was thinking of you this week, wondering how you're doing."

She looked up to see Emma's mother and father flanking her on either side. They looked a bit guarded, but Lucy couldn't blame them for that. "It's good to see you both, as well," she said. She stood up and offered her hand to Emma's dad, who shook it, but his head was on a swivel, keeping his eyes open to any possible threat to his daughter. Emma's mother leaned in and gave Lucy a quick hug. Lucy noted traces of dark circles under her eyes. She realized that both parents must be sleep-deprived and feeling unsafe out in public with Emma.

"It's good to see you too. We're not getting out as much as we used to, but Emma had her heart set on seeing the greatest pumpkin." The little girl's mom placed a protective hand on Emma's shoulder.

Lucy's heart went out to the little family. They'd been through so much, and since Emma had claimed to see her abductor at the festival, she imagined they were anxious most of the time.

"Emma, do you like to read?" Lucy asked.

"Of courths, I do! I'm a fatht reader!"

"Well, I'm wondering, if it's okay with your parents, if you might want to come to my bookstore sometime? We have story times for families where the moms and dads can come too. And we have a special Pumpkin Tea Party coming up Tuesday. I'd love it if you came. You can even be the autumn cookie fairy if you want and help me pass out the pumpkin cookies to all the little kids."

"Can I eat the cookieths too?"

Lucy laughed. "If it's okay with your parents, you can have as many cookies as they'll let you have."

Emma's parents sent silent signals of gratitude. She could tell that they loved the idea of having something special for their daughter to do in a contained environment. She gave them her phone number and suggested bringing Emma around at twelve-thirty to get dressed up and prepared for the part.

She watched Emma skip away with each parent holding one of her hands. Lucy tossed up an instinctual prayer that someday Emma and her family would feel safe and carefree again.

A large display of sunflowers caught Lucy's eye. The stems were cut and tied in bunches, but each bundle was at least five feet tall and contained several varieties of sunflower. The colors ranged from cream to yellow and gold, orange, mahogany, chocolate brown, and red. A few even had a purple hue that she'd never imagined possible for a sunflower. Also stunning were baskets of glass gem corn— with sparkling rainbow jewel-toned kernels. She made a mental note to come back later in the day to buy some of each for decorating the bookstore.

The band in the square was playing a jazzed-up version of a classic Halloween song and had the whole crowd dancing along. She worked her way around to the street corner behind the stage, where Hattie and the other ladies in charge had set up a hospitality tent. Lucy slipped inside and let her eyes adjust to the dim light until she spotted Hattie, Honey, and Glo sitting at a round table in the back. The three feisty women were howling with laughter.

"What's so funny?" she shouted. Even at that volume, Honey cupped a hand around her ear. "What are you all laughing about?" Lucy smiled at the women, hoping they'd let her in on whatever had cracked them up.

"Well, it's nothing, really—" Hattie began.

"It's no big thing," her grandmother started to say.

"It's the men! So competitive about the size of their pumpkins. A few of them have their self-esteem tied up in the size of their gourds!" Honey winked at Lucy with eyes full of mischief.

Lucy felt her face warm. She was sorry she'd asked!

"I see! Well, it's almost time for the winner to be announced. I'm gonna go wait for Mark out by the stage. Hattie, are you coming? I can try to save you all a spot if you want?"

"I'm on my way, Luce, but don't worry about saving a spot. The committee has chairs reserved right on the side of the stage. You go find Mark, and we'll meet up with you after."

Lucy smiled and nodded—and backed out of the tent. She wasn't sticking around to hear what else they might have to say about the poor pumpkin farmers.

Mark was waiting for her with Sam in tow. The three met up in the middle as the band was taking their final bow and the crowd was regrouping for the awards event. She reached up and gave Mark a kiss on this cheek and greeted Sam with a smile. She was looking forward to seeing what this year's pumpkin looked like and how big it was. Nearly every year, the largest pumpkin in the country was crowned at their small-town festival, a fact that the chamber of commerce and the town council were proud of.

A stir of excitement and whispers swept through the crowd as Mayor Alexander appeared on stage. Two men with official-looking tablets and clipboards joined the mayor. He cleared his throat in front of the microphone, causing an immediate hush.

"Welcome to The Greatest Pumpkin Contest!" The mayor smiled and waited for the cheers to die down. "We have a very exciting announcement this year. Before we reveal our winner, I'm overjoyed to tell you that our winner has shattered both state and national records! That means in addition to the state prize of ten thousand dollars, our winner today will also collect thirty-thousand dollars for the national prize and be recorded in *Guinness World Records.*"

The crowd broke out in massive cheering and clapping that took a few minutes to bring under control. Local camera crews filmed the announcement, probably hoping their national affiliates wanted to pick up the story. A couple of reporters fluffed their hair, getting ready to go live with a follow-up report as soon as the winner was announced.

"This year's winner is Johnny Jerome of Randolph Farms, with a whopping two-thousand-six-hundred-and-forty-four-pound giant monster!" The mayor pulled a lever, and a magenta curtain dropped, revealing a massive pumpkin on the back of a flatbed truck.

"Oh, my gourd!" Sam shouted, causing the people within the sound of his voice to laugh as everyone celebrated.

The line for pictures with the record-breaking pumpkin was two blocks long, and those who weren't queueing for selfies or taking pictures of their children posing with the behemoth vegetable were enjoying the party atmosphere. A new band started something dance-worthy, and food trucks rolled up, blowing the delicious scents of afternoon snacks and hinting at indulgent dinner offerings.

Lucy nabbed a bagful of fresh chocolate cream puffs before meeting Hattie at her car. Sam was already in the passenger seat, grinning. He rolled down the window. "Shotgun!"

The smirk disappeared from his face when Lucy held up the bag and said, "Cream puffs."

"That's not fair!" He looked to Hattie, who just shrugged.

He wavered and grumbled, but in the end, he vacated the seat and let Lucy have it. After she buckled in, he reached for the bag, but she put it out of his reach on the dash.

"Not yet, Sam. Wait until we get there so we can eat together. Mark's picking up coffee on the way." Mark had to return to his ship later, so he drove separately.

"Whatever." Sam stuck his lip out and pouted in the back seat, making Lucy laugh.

She waved her phone at them. "I got tickets already. We just have to pick them up at the counter." Going for a steam train ride was a plausible excuse for the four of them to meet and have a discussion away from everyone else. Chances were, they wouldn't be missed from the busy fall festival, but if anyone asked, they could claim it was a date or just say they needed some quiet after all the excitement.

Hattie pulled out onto the highway. It was only a five-minute drive to the train station, but Hattie was very cautious with her restored classic car—a red convertible with elaborate fins and polished chrome. The weather was nice, so she had the top down, and she'd wound her hair up in a scarf. Despite the seriousness of their errand, Lucy couldn't help but close her eyes and enjoy the sun on her face. Some days were just too perfect.

They pulled into an almost empty parking lot and parked a space over from Mark's truck. The attraction was often crowded—an antique railroad line that offered steam train rides through the redwood forest or to the beach and back—but today, they almost had the place to themselves. They walked down the path that led to a covered bridge. It stretched over a gentle stream filled with ducks and a frog or two.

Just beyond the bridge was a charming village meant to recreate an earlier era. Each building was a perfectly decorated miniature, from the post office to the livery stable and black smith's forge.

Mark picked up Lucy's hand, and they walked through to the boarding area of the Victorian-style station. Only a few families with small children waited on the wooden benches or played on the grass beside the platform. The next train was right on time, so they boarded without having to wait. Most of the families took a few minutes to board because the kids loved to see the big puffs of steam the engine let off as part of the show.

They chose a car halfway back along the train. Lucy was pretty sure they'd have it to themselves. She surveyed the interior, which was done up in rich red velvet and ornate wallpaper. Four sets of facing seats with tables between them furnished the fully enclosed car, unlike many of the other cars that were either open with running benches along the sides or traditional rows of seats with open windows. This car was far too stuffy to appeal to children.

The train got underway after a few minutes, and the four friends settled in around their table. Mark took a coffee out of the carrying tray and gave it to Lucy—he knew how she liked it prepared—and served Hattie next. Lucy headed Sam off with the first cream puff so he couldn't complain about special treatment. He grinned, mollified, but then he ruined it by smirking at Mark.

They took a few minutes to enjoy their treats and chat about the festival. The train would take half an hour to wind through the giant sequoias and climb the mountain, stopping at a scenic spot for hikers to depart from or for families to explore and share a picnic or just sit on one of the many benches scattered around the observation deck to soak up the beauty of the forest. The trains ran every forty-five minutes until closing, so people could just catch a different train for the trip down.

When the train stopped, they made their way to the observation deck below and then descended a curving staircase that took them down to a level area on the side of the mountain. It was perfect for sitting and taking in the view across the vast valley. Lucy looked up and smiled at a little boy peering over the edge of the railing above before his anxious mother pulled him back from the edge.

The place itself was so beautiful and idyllic that Lucy wished they hadn't come. It seemed wrong to spoil such a beautiful spot with talk of death and secrets and danger.

They filled Hattie in on what they'd found in the first room. Surprise registered on her face. She'd been a confidant and friend of Lucy's grandparents for decades, but they'd kept her and the others in their circle in the dark when it came to the details of what they were safeguarding. Hattie asked a few questions but didn't have a lot to offer. Lucy realized it was a lot to process.

They then brought her up to date on Cami's accusations and Andy's by-the-book behavior. Lucy laid out how concerned she was for their safety and her own. Hattie understood her reasoning—she'd lived through the same threats and danger Lucy had over the summer before her grandparents were rescued and returned from being presumed dead.

Lucy mentioned the second room she'd opened with Mark and only told the others that it appeared empty. She didn't mention the safe in the floor or the feeling of absolute dread she experienced in her brief time in the room.

She told them about the history she'd been reading in the journal. Hattie had heard parts of the story over the years, and Lucy had filled her in on what her grandfather told her after they rescued him, but she was surprised to hear about the ranch hand who killed one of Lucy's ancestors and was killed in turn by the victim's wife.

"I think that's a story we should leave in the past," Mark said.

Lucy couldn't agree more. It was part of her history, but it was long ago and a very different time. She only wished her grandparents had been more forthcoming about it with her.

"So, what's the plan now?" Hattie asked. "I'm not sure how any of this is going to help. You might find out everything you want to know, but what if it hurts your relationship with your grandparents?"

Lucy had considered that idea. She didn't want to damage

her bond with her family. "It's already not good. I overheard them talking. They don't trust me and don't like me snooping around. I know they've been through a lot, and I know they want to protect me. But I lost them once already and I can't do that again. I don't think they understand how dangerous it is to keep all these secrets and keep us in the dark at the same time. I can't help them if I don't know what I'm trying to protect them from or why it's all happening again."

Mark stroked her back. "I really thought everything was over after we caught Officer Franklin and his father and got your grandparents back safe and sound. But now it doesn't seem it was limited to just one small group of people who know something and are coming after some part of what your family has hidden." He shook his head as if trying to shake away a memory. "I can't stand the idea of you being in danger again—any of you."

She could see how earnest he was, and she loved him for it. "I want all of us to be safe. Truthfully, I think someday soon, the secrets will come out. They'll have to, and then the burden of trying to protect the secrets will be lifted. They're not worth even a single life being lost."

Sam, who'd been quiet until now, squirmed on the bench. "So, when are we going back to the basement? It seems to me there are a couple more rooms we should check out."

"I think we should plan for Tuesday. It's a busy day at the bookstore. The Pumpkin Tea Party is the perfect cover for each of you to be there as volunteers. In the meantime, I'll keep reading through the journals to see if I can find anything else that might help us."

"Speaking of that which might help us, Andy told me something interesting." Sam waited until everyone was focused on him. "They're dismissing Cami's complaint about Lucy. There's no evidence, and Cami has been found to be an unreliable character. Surprisingly, she is using her real name, but Andy was clear that little else she told us was true. He thinks she met the pastor impersonator—make that the im*parson*ator—through the university he worked for. He was on sabbatical and told colleagues he planned to return with some ground-breaking research. What we don't know is why she was pretending to be his daughter. When Andy went to interview her yesterday, she was nowhere to be found."

"She's gone missing again?" Lucy rolled her eyes hard enough that it hurt. "Somebody check the root cellar." She barked out a small laugh. "All we know for sure is that she's up to no good! Did Andy tell you anything more about her?"

"No, he did say he's following up some interesting leads, though. I don't know how I was so blind. I thought she was genuinely interested in me, but now I'm worried she was just using me to get to you and your grandparents."

"Don't worry about that, Sam. You deserve to be happy, and you had no reason to think she was anything other than what she said she was. We'll figure it out."

"Speaking of figuring it out, we should probably get back. The last train will be here in a few minutes. If we miss it, it's a long hike down the fire road to get back to where we parked." Mark offered his hand to Hattie, who took it and pulled herself up. She stretched for a moment and then patted him on the cheek before heading up the stairs.

Mark offered his arm to Lucy, and she was happy to take it. "We'll figure it all out together. We make a good team, all of us. We just need to avoid getting caught."

A slight breeze played around on the upper platform, picking up yellow leaves and swirling them into a dancing, golden vortex. Lucy watched with delight until something moved on the edge of her vision. When she turned to look, there was nothing there. A cold shiver worked its way across her shoulders, and she hurried to climb back on board the train.

nxious thoughts crowded Lucy's mind, and she kept cycling through them. She missed Mark when he was on the cutter. He loved being out on the open ocean with its many wonders and moods, but she was restless for his return. The sooner they could get into the other rooms downstairs, the better. Cami was still missing, but Lucy had a hunch the woman was nearby and hiding. Lucy's grandparents weren't being overtly unkind, but she hated the feeling of being at odds and the distance between them.

She spent her morning gathering supplies and baking cookies for the Pumpkin Tea Party the next day. Over the summer, she'd put together a fairy garden tea party that was, by all accounts, an unequaled success. It also ended up being a great marketing tool. This time, her attention would be divided, though, as she and Mark planned to slip away to the other compass rooms. Hattie and Sam would be on hand to help keep her grandparents diverted.

She had just pulled a batch of chocolate chip pumpkin cookies from the oven when someone knocked on the back door. Lucy slid them onto a cooling rack and peeked out the window. Gracie stood there, waving cheerfully, so Lucy unlocked the door and invited her in.

"You're killing me, Lucy!" Gracie said. "The smell of those cookies almost made me fall off my ladder!"

Lucy laughed since her friend appeared unharmed. "I'm so sorry. Can I make it up to you? How about some tea and cookies?"

"I thought you'd never ask! I need to wash my hands. Be right back." She headed out of the kitchen to the small guest bath dedicated for the use of bookstore patrons.

Lucy put the kettle on to boil and pulled out a selection of autumnal teas, some cups and spoons, plus small plates for the cookies. The ones just out of the oven still needed to cool, but she had plenty from a previous batch ready to eat. She was pleased. It would be nice to have something like a normal chat with a friend in her cozy kitchen.

Before Gracie returned, though, Lucy heard her grandmother's voice in the dining room. "You there. What are you doing?" Her voice was sharp, so Lucy hurried into the other room.

Gracie stood in the doorway between the dining room and the bookstore, her hands open and shoulders bunched up in a shrug. Glo was glaring at Gracie as if she were a shoplifter—or worse.

"I was just coming back from the bathroom. Lucy made cookies . . ." Gracie appeared to be confused. "Did I do something to upset you?"

Glo looked back and forth between Lucy and her friend, her eyes narrowed to slits and mouth pinched in apparent suspicion.

"Where did you come from?" Glo asked. "And don't tell me the bathroom. I didn't see you come in, and now you're wandering around the house."

"Grandma!" Lucy couldn't believe her ears. "What's wrong with you? She's my friend!"

"I came by to check the trim in the back of the house. It's finished. But I wanted to make sure it dried well and had good coverage. And that everything was cleaned up properly. I put the thirty-six-foot ladder back in Mr. Patterson's shop and locked the door. I was on my way out when I smelled Lucy's cookies and thought I'd say hello."

"And I'm glad you did!" Lucy turned to her grandmother. "We're just about to have some tea and cookies. Would you like to join us?"

"What? No, I'm working in the bookstore. I just thought . . . Well, I just thought she was trying to sneak into the house from the bookstore." She gave Gracie a long look and said, "I'm sorry. We just can't be too careful these days. You girls go ahead. Enjoy your cookies." Glo stalked off back into the bookstore.

"I am so sorry. I don't know what's gotten into her lately." Lucy reached for her friend and pulled her back into the kitchen. "I've been wanting to catch up with you anyway. I feel like I've barely seen you."

After they settled into the chairs and Lucy poured the tea, Tor nosed his way in through the cat door and went straight to Gracie. He stood up on his back legs and sniffed her for a moment, and then with surprising grace, jumped into her lap, where he curled into a circle and started purring.

"Looks like you made a friend," Lucy said.

"I really hope I have." Gracie gave Lucy a warm smile. "Loyal, kind friends are the greatest treasure."

Lucy's smile faltered, but just for a second. "I agree. Here's to loyal, kind friends! Cheers!"

Tuesdays were half-days for the schools in Seaview. Guardians picked children up at noon from their various campuses, and any event that promised to entertain or even keep the kids busy was always popular. Lucy had planned the day's events with her grandparents' blessing—they'd heard all about the success of the fairy garden tea party over the summer and were curious to see how it would work.

She'd let them know that there would be several volunteers coming to help, including Mark, Sam, Hattie, a few of the teens who'd volunteered for her in the past, and Gracie. She made sure her grandparents knew that Emma and her parents were coming, and she wanted to make the day special for the little girl who'd already been through so much. Lucy failed to mention that she'd be using the tea party as cover so she could slip into the basement and see what else was hidden in the compass rooms.

Her grandmother told her that Allen Morgan would also be on the grounds at some point in the afternoon to finish up the instillation of the additional surveillance equipment. Lucy didn't think it would be disruptive, though, as most of the work was on the perimeter of the property or on the exterior of the house.

Gracie had been happy to volunteer, even though she wasn't privy to Lucy's ulterior motives. She was keen to see Emma again and loved the idea of giving her VIP treatment. Gracie volunteered to be a "lady in waiting" for Emma to help her dress up and told Lucy she also planned to find something fun to wear in the oversized box of costumes and accessories. Lucy was in favor of that idea and had gathered more options so all the teens could dress up as well. Kai was bringing his little sister. He'd want to make it special for her too.

Hattie was the first to arrive, bringing an early lunch for the volunteers and a lot more cookies for the party—a combination of trays from her café and Honey's Bakery. She added them to the table Lucy had already half-filled with cookies of her own.

"You didn't have to do this!" Lucy said.

"I'm happy to. Besides, you're gonna need every bit of it. I overheard some parents talking, and it sounds like the whole town plans to show up!"

Lucy was beginning to worry that things weren't going as she planned. Crowd control would be an issue if Hattie was right. The bookstore could only hold so many people at a time. When Mark showed up a few minutes later with Sam and a couple of the teen boys, she put them to work dragging lawn games out of the storage room, including the popular foam swords she'd kept from their summer event. At least that way, there'd be some activities for those who weren't inside for cookies and books yet.

Gracie arrived next, and Lucy was delighted to see her in full costume already. She wore a peasant blouse and a colorful broomstick skirt with knee-high leather boots and a brown suede cowboy hat. She carried a battery-operated jack-o'-lantern that shifted colors and matched her dangling pumpkin earrings.

"Now *that's* what I'm talking about!" She hugged her friend and made her twirl around a few times to get the full effect. "The kids are going to love you!" Lucy gave her the rundown on the games and activities and showed her where the cookies were set up. There was a crown and a throne waiting for Emma, along with a box of costumes to choose from. She'd set up a space in the office area of the storage room for Emma to get dressed. Gracie would be there to help her. Then the doors would open, and the fun would begin.

She looked to Mark for reassurance and felt her heart warm when he gave her a goofy two-thumbs-up. Surely, that was a good sign that things were going to go well, right?

Lucy had picked up the journals again the night before,

flipping through them at random. Several times, she found references to things she didn't understand—each of the writers seemed to share the same code and were unwilling to say outright what they were guarding. Setting her worries aside, she took comfort in the thought that she'd soon have access to the knowledge she needed and be able to figure out a way to keep her friends and family safe.

Just before the event was scheduled to start, Lucy's grandfather came to find her. "You need to see this. Come out on the porch with me."

She followed him through the store, stopping to give Tor some scritches on his high shelf perch. He was smart enough to know when to stay out of the fray. When she stepped outside, she felt a little jolt of shock. There were kids everywhere. Many of them had arrived in costume and looked ready to do mischief. She could feel her orderly plans going out the window in the face of barely restrained chaos. Parents milled around, and a line to enter the bookstore already wound down the driveway and a little way down the block. She was blown away. How on earth had her little cookies and books event turned into a major draw?

"Right. Go inside and get Mark and Sam and Hattie for me, please." She nodded to her grandfather, motioning him back inside, and he hurried to comply.

She scanned the crowd until her eyes landed on Kai. He was horsing around with some of the other teens on the lawn. She recognized a few of who'd been volunteers for her in the summer. She whistled once and shouted his name, causing him to look up and make eye contact. She waved him over.

"Hey, Lucy! S'up?" he asked.

"This"—she motioned all around them—"is way more than I bargained for. Would you like to earn some extra cash? I could really use some help. I know your sister is here, but she could hang out with Gracie and Emma."

"I mean, I'm happy to help. You don't have to pay me. What do you need?"

"Well, we'll talk about payment later. I'm hoping that you and some of the other teens would run a few rounds of the LARP game we did in the summer, but you could change it up to be Halloween-themed groups, like magical beings versus monsters—something like that. In the meantime, I'm going to have some of the guys bring the food outside because there's no way this crowd will work indoors."

Kai's eyes lit up. "I'm in. I know everybody is going to want to help. And I think my sister would love to hang out with Emma and Gracie. Let me go get her, and then I'll get the guys going, and we'll just start the games now."

"Thanks, Kai. That would be amazing."

Hattie came out with Mark and Sam, followed by Lucy's grandparents.

"Oh, my word!" she said. "We're going to need reinforcements!"

"To say the least! Mark, Sam, can you bring the tables out of the storage room and set them up out here on the side? And then grab some folks and have them help you move all the cookie trays out here, but put someone in charge of holding off the crowds. Grandma, you might be perfect for that."

Her grandmother gave her a speculative look but nodded. "That sounds fine. I've been wanting to see one of those famous LARP battles. So many people made a point to tell me what great ideas you had."

Kai brought his sister to Lucy and introduced her. "Lolly, this is Miss Lucy. You remember her, right?" The little girl nodded, making her blonde curls bob up and down. "And this is Miss Gracie."

Lolly's eyes lit up, and she said, "Wow. Are you a cowgirl pumpkin princess?"

Gracie laughed. "Something like that! You're going to hang out with me and another little girl named Emma." She pointed down the driveway. "Lucy, I think our little guest is stuck in line! I should go get her." She extended her hand to Lolly. "Want to come with me? Then we can go check out the costume box and get all decked out!"

"Thanks, Gracie. I appreciate your overseeing the cookie fairy princesses today!" She winked at Lolly.

"Best. Day. Ever!" Lolly celebrated with a fist pump. "Yeehaw!"

Everyone did their part—Mark and Sam moved the tables and cookies outside, Gracie and the girls headed inside to the storage room to get ready, and Kai already had three teams of fighting factions grouped together and advancing on their enemies. Lucy laughed as one little girl charged out ahead of her group with soft brown hair and an emerald green cape flying behind her. She let out a wild war cry, a look of sheer exhilaration on her face as she lived out her foam-sword battle fantasy.

"Lucy, I just had a call from the doc. The city has a whole truckload of small pumpkins left over from the festival, and he wants to know if it's okay to bring them here for the kids to take home." Hattie raised an eyebrow and shrugged. "What should I tell him?"

"Tell him to have them come in the back gate from the community garden and just drive right over on the grass. There's no way they'll get through that crowd of kids in the driveway."

She waggled her phone at Lucy and said, "Already did. Great minds think alike!"

Lucy pulled Mark aside in the dining room and told him about the pumpkin delivery. He agreed that the more going on, the better, to keep everyone occupied while they snuck away downstairs.

"Hattie's going to tell anyone who asks that I've gone to change. You go out and direct the city guys to unload in front of where the summer house used to be, then come in the back door and meet me downstairs. I'll go ahead and move some boxes while I wait for you."

"Sounds like a plan." He kissed her quickly. "See you in a few."

*Chapter
Twenty-Four*

Mark was a long time in coming. Lucy managed to move the boxes away from both remaining doors, and he still hadn't come downstairs. She tried texting him, but there was no answer. She debated waiting a few more minutes but decided she should just go ahead and open the rooms herself. If something had come up, she was sure he was trying to handle it so she could go forward. Mark wouldn't want her to wait, she felt sure.

She opened the south-facing door next with the key marked *Meridionalis*. The light came on as she pushed the door in. There was nothing in the room except a large vault-style safe, akin to something a bank would have. The door was open, revealing a room with many safety deposit boxes. There was also a small table and two chairs in the vault, where someone could examine the contents of a container.

She hesitated, then stepped inside. She had a fear of being closed in, though, so she turned one of the chairs over and laid it across the corner of the entry. The first set of boxes were open and empty, but the majority were closed and locked. She could see that the room key was far too large to open anything in the vault, so she backed out and returned the chair to its original position. She would have to confront her grandparents later about the safe and its contents. Nothing that she and Sam had looked over from the estate mentioned any of this, nor were any keys or information about the things stored in the compass rooms included in the boxes she'd inherited when they were declared deceased. Lucy was a bit peeved. She didn't care about whatever money or treasures they had stored. It was just the idea that they'd left her in the dark and vulnerable by not planning for whatever this was.

She closed the room and crossed over to the last door. It was built into the east wall. All the other doors were centered, but this one was off by just enough to make her wonder. She put the *Orientalis* key into the door and turned it. It didn't unlock in the same way as the others had—instead, a series of clicks and pings sounded as gears and tumblers went into motion. A faint hiss of compressed air preceded the door finally unlocking.

Wary now, she pushed the door open a few inches. Nothing happened, and no lights came on, so she pushed in a little farther and turned on her phone light. She was glad she had because the floor angled steeply away from the door. Anyone who tried to step inside to find a light switch would have rolled an ankle and gone tumbling downhill.

She pushed the door all the way open and scanned the walls. There wasn't a light switch, but there was a small landing attached to the wall on the right side of the door. She had to hang on to the door frame and swing herself around to stand on it, and when she did, she could see it was a primitive stone stair-case that led to the bottom of the room. The floor near the far wall was a complete story lower than the floor she'd come in on.

Lucy made her way down the stairs and picked her way to the far wall. She could just make out a rusted iron door tucked into the corner. It didn't look as though it had moved in ages. She passed her light over the handle. There was a keyhole, but it looked as if rust or debris had filled it up. She decided to give the handle a yank anyway.

The door didn't budge, but after a few seconds, a small panel in the wall opened to reveal a black box with a glowing green screen. A message flashed across the screen and disappeared. It had instructed her to place her palm down on the surface, so she did. She didn't expect the print scanner to recognize her, but after scanning, the screen went dark, and the iron door swung silently inward.

She was trying to wrap her head around the incongruity of a high-tech yet antique door when she heard a noise from above. Thinking Mark had come, at last, Lucy looked up and warned, "Watch out, that's not a step!" She didn't want him to stumble and fall.

"Luthy?" A little girl's voice called out to her.

"Emma? Is that you? Stay right there, sweetheart. The floor is dangerous!" She shone her light up to where Emma stood on the threshold. "Don't come any closer, sweetie. You should go back upstairs!"

"I can't. I have to hide. He'th here." Emma's voice cracked with terror.

"I'm coming to get you. Just hang on." Lucy retraced her steps as fast as she dared could in the near darkness and climbed the stairs two at a time. "Where's Gracie? She should be with you."

"She wath. She put me in the bathement door and told me to hide. She thaid she would come back for me."

Lucy couldn't imagine what had happened in the half hour or so that she'd been downstairs, but she reached Emma and told her to hold her hand as she scooped her over to the landing beside the door. Lucy realized the floor was a trap, intended to catch someone who wasn't meant to be there unawares. She would have to talk to her grandparents because she could have been hurt—let alone an innocent like Emma could have been injured.

Lucy checked her phone. No messages from Mark or anyone, but she only had a single bar of connectivity down there. She pushed down a wave of nausea. How on earth had the man who'd abducted Emma before found her here? Was he stalking her?

"Okay, listen. I want you to be very quiet. We're going to hide. I'm not going to let anything happen to you. Just hold on to me, and we're going to go down here, and nobody will be able to get us, okay?"

The little girl nodded, but Lucy was sure she was in shock. She shot off a text to Mark and started to push the door closed. Without the special compass keys, no one would be able to get in. Before the door closed, though, someone jammed a boot into the space between the door and the jamb. Emma yelped and buried her face in Lucy's side.

"Emma? It's me. Gracie!" The boot was followed by an arm pushing the door open.

Relief flooded Lucy, but it still took a second or two for her to catch her breath and answer.

"Gracie, I've got Emma. Watch out. There's no floor in front of you. I'm going to shine my light on the landing, okay?"

"I see it. Hang on." Gracie made the jump over and stood huddled with Lucy and Emma on the now-crowded top step. She reached behind her and shut the door gently.

"Come on, follow me." Lucy led Emma and Gracie down the stairs and across the room with her phone light. It wasn't much light, but enough to get them there without tripping. The iron door stood open, waiting, and there was nothing but darkness beyond.

"Lucy, what is this place?" Gracie asked.

"Never mind that. Tell me what happened and why Emma ended up in the basement looking for a place to hide. She said that man is here." Emma whimpered, so Lucy wrapped both arms around her. "Don't worry, sweetie, we're not going to let anyone near you."

"I think we should make sure we're somewhere secure before we discuss—things. How sturdy is the door up there?"

Lucy knew what she was asking. "Well, it's pretty sturdy. You need special keys to open it." She thought about it a moment longer. If someone really wanted to get in and wasn't afraid of making a lot of noise, they could. With all the activity going on around the place today, the noise would go unnoticed. "This door here, though, this door is so sturdy not even a dragon could get in."

Gracie caught on. "Well, if a dragon can't get in, I guess we'd be safe in there?"

"Let me see if I can find the lights, and then we'll go inside. I'm guessing this might be the safest place in the whole house." Lucy worried about exposing her family's secrets—whatever they were—to her new friend, but she reminded herself no treasure is worth even a single life being lost or a single hair on a child's head being harmed.

She directed her phone's light inside the room, but it didn't penetrate the darkness very far. The floor looked okay—no surprises on this side. She leaned inside and looked at the walls on either side of the door until she located the light switch.

"I'm going to turn the lights on after we're inside, okay? That way, no one will see any light and know where we went." Lucy was pretty sure the light wouldn't show under the outer door, but she didn't want to take a chance.

Together, Gracie and Lucy walked Emma through the door, and Lucy closed it behind them. Lucy reached across and turned on the light switch. She gasped in surprise as light after light turned on, farther and farther down a long passageway. The roof was beam work, and the walls a few yards beyond where they stood were rough stone.

Emma had had enough. She sat down on the floor and burst into tears. "I want my mom!"

Gracie sat down next to her and pulled her into her lap. "It's going to be okay, chickadee. We're going to get you back to your mom as fast as possible, right Lucy?"

Lucy nodded, but something had caught her eye. There was another door hidden in the rock. She couldn't help herself. She had to know. What on earth could be worth all this—all this secrecy, all the effort into hiding something and keeping everyone out—what could be worth all this *trouble?* She walked up to the door and tried the handle. It didn't budge. Of course, it wouldn't.

Then she heard the click of a lock turning and heard a mechanical voice say, "Recognized, Lucy Patterson." It was followed by a whir that caused her to look up. A camera focused on her face. She supposed her grandparents had done some preparation after all in case they passed away before letting her in on the family secrets.

She pushed the door open. She had to know. The light came on as the door opened, shining from above, focused on three glass display cases. The first one held a large coin, suspended as if standing up on its edge. The second one held a thin, golden rod with an exquisite, carved rose made of dark pink gemstone, and at its center glittered an enormous diamond. It was elegant in its simplicity but stunning in design. The third case held—on a velvet pillow—a medieval crown of gold, inlaid with large rubies, emeralds, and diamonds.

"Oh my . . ." Lucy started.

"*Dios mio,*" Gracie added.

"What the heck?" Emma finished.

What the heck, indeed! Lucy's mind scrambled for an answer, but she came up with exactly nothing.

Chapter
Twenty-Five

I don't think we should be in here." Gracie pulled Emma out
of the room and waited.

"Luthy?" Emma called for her when she didn't follow them.

Lucy felt mesmerized. *This is next level. How is it possible my
grandparents have kept this a secret and somehow had access to such
high-tech security equipment?* The camera had scanned her face and
used some sort of facial recognition system to give her access.
She worried about the consequences of opening the door. The
access must have been logged on a computer somewhere, and a
notification sent. At this point, she hoped that was the case. *I'd
like nothing better than to have my grandparents know where I am and
what I've seen.*

She shook off the avalanche of questions threatening to
overwhelm her mind. Keeping Emma safe had to be the priority,
so she took a final look at the objects in the room as she made
her way out. She noticed some words on the back side of the
coin as she passed by it: NON SUFFICIT ORBIS. For some reason,
the phrase made her head hurt. Her Latin was rusty—she'd have
to look it up later.

She came out and closed the door behind her, agreeing with
Gracie. They shouldn't be in there. She leaned down to Emma's
level and made eye contact. "I think we're safe down here."

The little girl wrapped her arms around Lucy's neck and held on tight, so Lucy picked her up and shifted her onto her hip. She gestured for Gracie to follow as she walked down the tunnel.

Lucy had no idea where the tunnel went, but it had electric lights, and the floor had been smoothed at some point in time. She guessed that the tunnel led somewhere from which they could escape. She wanted to know how things unfolded, but Emma was calm for the moment, and she didn't want to further upset her by asking a lot of questions.

Gracie seemed to be thinking along the same lines. "Oh, Lucy, did you know Kai's sister is helping him with the games? She's on team Magical Beings, and they won the first round."

Lucy let out a little bit of breath she didn't know she'd been holding and nodded. Gracie was letting her know that Kai's sister was safe and that whatever happened, she'd already gone back to play with the other kids beforehand.

"That sounds fun. Is team Knights in Shining Armor winning against team Monsters?" Lucy tried to keep her tone light and casual.

"Well, that round hadn't started yet, but I sent Miss Hattie a text and told her I wanted to know the outcome. I'm rooting for the Knights. You can never underestimate a good knight." Gracie gave Lucy a wink.

"I guess we'll find out soon enough. I sent Mark a text, too, right before you joined us. I had low bars, so I'm not completely sure it went through, but I know he was planning to come and tell me who was winning."

Emma raised her head from Lucy's shoulder and looked at both of them. "You are not very good at thith. You can thay it. You don't have to talk in code. I'm not a baby."

She was so earnest that Lucy couldn't help but kiss her

cheek. "You're right. You're brave and strong. We didn't want to upset you. I'm sorry."

"I'm sorry too," Gracie said. "You really are brave, and you saved yourself. You saw him, and you ran back to me, and you went into the basement all by yourself to hide while I sent Miss Hattie a message. I took a picture too. Can I show it to you?"

Emma nodded, so Gracie pulled up the photo she'd taken of the man she thought was coming after Emma. "Is that him?"

Emma indicated she wanted to get down, so Lucy set her back on her feet. She took the phone from Gracie and zoomed in on the picture. "That'th him. That'th the bad man."

Lucy took the phone next. "Are you sure? I know him. He's here installing security cameras for my grandparents."

"I'm sure. That'th the man that took me when we were camping, and he put me in the woodth. And he thaid if I moved, he would kill my mom." Tears welled up in Emma's eyes.

"Oh, sweetie. I believe you! Now that we know who it is, we'll have Captain Andy take him away and lock him up for good!"

Emma nodded and took Lucy's hand. "I like Captain Andy. He gave me a big teddy bear at the hothpital. Ith he on team Knight in Shining Armor?"

"Definitely!" Lucy laughed. "My boyfriend, Mark, is his son, and he is also on that team."

Emma looked up and smiled. "I think girlth can be knighth too. And we can save the boys just as much as they thave us."

Gracie leaned over and gave the little girl a squeeze. "You are more right than you know, little one! Some of the best dragon slayers are girls."

"My mom thays princehesses have to save themselves these days. But I told her it's okay if we all save each other." Emma beamed at them. "We are thaving each other right now, right?"

"You know it!" Lucy said.

"I have such hope for the future, *chula*. Little girls like you make the world a better place." Gracie reached for Emma's other hand. "What do you say? Let's get out of here. I'm kind of hungry for a nice meal of roasted dragon."

Emma growled. "Me too! Come on, Lucy, let'th go kick some dragon butt."

They'd walked for another ten minutes or so before the tunnel branched off. One side curved away and went deeper underground. A chain and what looked like a gold rush-era mining cart barred the entrance. *That's a mystery for another day,* Lucy thought. They continued straight along the main passage for a few more minutes before it began to climb uphill.

"This is good," Gracie said. "Up probably means out!"

At the end of the tunnel, a set of stone stairs led to a door. Lucy went up first, in case it was a security door that wanted her fingerprint or to scan her face. The door appeared to be just a normal steel door. It would be difficult to break into but didn't seem to have any extra security measures. She gave the door a tug, but it was locked. Without a key, they would have to walk back the long way. Doing that might put them in a dangerous situation in the basement.

On a whim, Lucy pulled out the keyring to the compass rooms and tried it in the lock. It slid in, and she started to turn the key. However, before she could, the door opened from the other side.

Lucy jumped back, fighting to keep her footing. Standing in the doorway with a grin like the Cheshire cat was none other than her grandmother. Behind her stood Miss Honey, which made no sense at all until Lucy's nose filled with the scent of fresh bread and cinnamon and vanilla.

"Grandma? Miss Honey? We're at the bakery?"

"We've been waiting for you. Come through. We have a lot to discuss. Gracie, you and Emma come on up. Honey has some special cinnamon buns waiting for you."

"What? No cinnamon bun for me?" Lucy asked.

"It depends. We'll have to see about that. But for now, we need to get Emma back to her parents." Her grandmother stepped aside so they could file into a room in the bakery's basement. Once they were all in, Honey locked the door. Then she and Glo pushed a cabinet in front of it, obscuring the fact that there was anything other than a wall there.

"Come on, Emma, let's get you cleaned up." Honey reached for the little girl, but instead of complying, she pulled her hand back.

"I don't know you. I'm thtaying with Lucy and Gracie. They're my friendth."

Lucy believed the stubborn set of her jaw meant she was prepared to dig in. "It's okay. Miss Honey is our friend. She's really nice. You can go with her."

"No. I'm not going with her. She'th a Boomer." She crossed her arms in a show of stubbornness.

Lucy had to bite down to keep from laughing at hearing the tiny girl use tween slang like that.

Glo sputtered. "I need to talk to Lucy. In my day, little girls did as they were told."

"In your day, little girlth didn't have choices. It'th my day, not your day, and I am *not* going anywhere without my friends."

Honey couldn't hold it in any longer and let out a peal of laughter. "She's right, Glo. You can't make her do anything. Also, I remember when we were girls, and you pretty much never did as you were told!"

"Oh, whatever!" Glo bent down to Emma's eye level and said, "I like my girls feisty, and you're as sassy as they come. We'll all go together."

Five minutes later, Emma's face and hands were clean, and she was devouring a cinnamon roll with Gracie. The two sat next to each other, heads together, having what appeared to be an intense conversation.

"Right now, what you need to know is that Emma's safe. Hattie got the text and understood what was going on, and Mark was able to tell us where you were. We caught Allen Morgan red-handed. He was in the basement trying to pry one of the doors open. Andy and Mark took him to the police station. Emma's going to have to make a statement, and Gracie too. But we need to minimize our exposure. We'll talk about what you did later, but for now, I'm hoping we can convince those two to keep what they saw to themselves.

"We also need to smuggle you three back to the property without being seen, so we're going to ride in Honey's delivery van. We have to go as soon as possible. Emma's parents are melting down. We told them there are old lava tunnels on the property and that we have people checking them and searching for Emma. Andy has his deputies out looking, too, so we need to be careful. Do you think they'll go along with it?"

Lucy was troubled. She hated the need to cover things up and keep secrets this way, especially if it meant asking other people to lie. Before she could answer, Emma and Gracie walked over to the table where Lucy and her grandmother were sitting.

"I have thomething to thay."

Lucy repressed a smile. This kid was too sweet for her own good.

"I'm listening," Glo said.

"I know we thaw things that were hidden for a reason. I'm not going to tell anyone what I thaw, ever. Knights have a code of honor, and I'm a knight, just like Lucy and Gracie. We will keep the thecret, I promise."

Glo looked up at Gracie to confirm.

"That's right. As far as I'm concerned, Emma told me that the bad man was after her, so I took a snapshot and sent it to Hattie and then went after Emma. I found her in a tunnel, safe but afraid, and then Lucy found us and brought us back." Gracie put a hand on Emma's shoulder. "Lucy is our friend, and we will protect her, right?"

Emma nodded. "Yeth. We are dragon-butt-kickers. Gracie thays I am an onery knight with her."

Glo laughed. "Did she say honorary or onery? Because I could see it going both ways."

"Don't listen to her, Emma. Of course, you are a knight in shining armor, and it's not even honorary as far as I'm concerned. You are a real knight!"

Emma shook her head. "Not yet, I thtill need to be thworn in. Gracie says I have to grow a few more years before then, but she will teach me all about being a knight."

Emma was being serious, so Lucy decided to go along. "I'm sure you will continue to grow in all your good character qualities, like bravery and loyalty and kindness. You will make a wonderful knight, and any group of knights would be honored to have you."

"Thankth, Lucy." Emma was radiating happiness. "I'm only joining one, though. The Order of Montetha."

"I've never heard of the Order of Montetha, but I'm sure it's a good one." Lucy patted the little girl's cheek.

In slow motion, Glo pushed her chair back and stood, facing Gracie. Lucy was close enough to see the hair was standing up on her grandmother's arms, and her face was a mixture of surprise and fear.

A small sound escaped Glo's throat as she tried to back up. Lucy couldn't understand what was happening and reached an arm out to steady her grandmother.

"You . . . You're . . ." Glo stammered.

"Grandma, what's wrong?" Lucy stood up, afraid her grandmother was having a cardiac episode or worse.

Gracie responded. "I am." She gave Lucy a warm smile. "It's okay. I'm not a threat. Emma was trying to say Montesa, but her lisp is the cutest thing."

Lucy's grandmother seemed far from relieved. If anything, she was even paler than before. Lucy put an arm around her shoulders to brace her because she looked as if she might pass out.

"Gracie, what's going on? Why is my grandmother looking at you that way? What are you both not telling me?"

"I'll fill you in on everything, Lucy. But first, we need to get Emma back to her parents. We've agreed on what to tell them, all true things but nothing that leaves you exposed, and I honestly don't think they will push about any of it." Gracie turned to Honey, who'd busied herself with taking things out of the ovens and turning them off. "If you're ready, I think we should go now."

Everything had gone to plan. Emma told her parents and the deputies just what they'd rehearsed, and she insisted on giving Lucy and Gracie multiple hugs before letting her parents take her home. She also went home with an entire box of cookies from Hattie, and she was in such good spirits that it seemed to help her parents calm down a bit.

Now that the danger was past and her abductor was safely behind bars, Lucy was hopeful the young parents would find a way to feel normal again. Emma made her parents promise to bring her back to the bookstore to visit and to let her see Gracie and Lucy sometimes. Both women assured her parents that they'd love nothing better and that they were very fond of Emma.

Most people hadn't realized anything was wrong, and by all accounts, the event was a big hit. Kai and the teens had pretty much taken over everything: games, activities, passing out cookies, and helping kids select pumpkins. She made a mental note to throw a big pizza party for the teens as soon as possible to thank them for all their help and hard work.

The table was set, and Hector had dropped off a large order a few minutes before. Hattie had called it in when Lucy texted Mark to let them know they were on the way.

Glo had gone to lie down, which Lucy guessed to mean she wanted to talk to Ulyss alone and fill him in. Lucy was tired of being in the dark, but seeing how shaken her grandmother was, she was willing to wait just a little bit longer for answers.

Gracie stuck around to help but wasn't willing to answer any questions until those who needed to hear her story were together. It was not, she said, a tale she would tell twice. Gracie worked on unboxing the food and transferring it to platters and bowls while Lucy went outside and lit the propane heaters stationed near each side of the outdoor dining table. Lucy turned on the twinkle lights that illuminated the lawn and patio. It was magical with the backdrop of giant redwood trees that rimmed the yard.

She hoped good food and a pleasant atmosphere would help to get people in the right frame of mind for what was sure to be a difficult conversation ahead. She decided to just put pitchers of water on the table and set up the coffee and tea carafes on the patio. This wasn't the sort of night where wine with dinner would be a good idea.

Lucy heard Mark's truck coming up the driveway. Her heart beat a little faster as she rounded the corner of the house and waved him over. His face lit up when he saw her, and in two big steps, he had her in his arms.

"Lucy, I was so worried! I'm so glad you're all right." He kissed her cheeks and then pretended to look her over. "You are all right, right?"

"I'm fine! Everything worked out. But what happened to you today? I thought you were right behind me."

"Well, I was, but your grandmother caught me about to go back in the house and asked me to bring a chair outside for her to sit on. Then she wanted a drink of water. Finally, she admitted that she suspected I was trying to sneak in to see you and that you were getting dressed, and it wasn't proper. She accused me of shenanigans under her roof, Luce. I told her truthfully that no shenanigans had occurred, and she had nothing to worry about."

"I'm going to tell her to mind her own business!" Lucy felt the warmth creeping up her cheeks.

"No, don't worry about it. She's just set in her ways." He kissed her lightly on the lips. "If we get up to anything, we'll just be careful not to tell her." He winked.

She knew he was kidding. "Deal," Lucy said. "Did you get the text I sent?"

"The one that said: East, Emma, Hiding? I did, but I didn't get it till much later. Right after I got free from your grandmother, Andy called me. He had some bad news. They found Cami—but she didn't make it."

"What? Where?" Lucy clutched Mark's shirt and tried to take a deep breath. She felt lightheaded and in urgent need of a chair. Mark scooped her up and sat her on one of the patio chairs.

"Are you okay? I'm sorry. I didn't mean to upset you. Andy said he thought you might be upset about it."

"No, I'm okay. It's just been a day. A really long day, and there's still so much I need to tell you. But tell me what happened to Cami."

"Well, we know now that she was killed by the same person who killed the pastor, er, professor. And that person is the same one who abducted Emma."

Lucy's head was swimming. "How do you know this?"

"Let me explain what happened. When I got off the phone with Andy, I came to look for you. Before I even made it into the house, Hattie forwarded me a text from Gracie with the picture of Allen Morgan and the message that he was Emma's abductor and was chasing her now. I made a beeline for the basement, where I found him trying to pry open one of the compass room doors. He had a lock-picking kit, but that didn't work, so he was using a fireman's Halligan bar to try to pound the door open. He would have eventually gotten in that way.

"So, I knocked him down and held him. I was going to try to call for help, but I didn't have to. Your suspicious grandmother followed me and called the station. She brought me zip ties, Luce. She had zip ties!"

Lucy giggled, not because the idea of Mark fighting with a homicidal maniac was funny, it was just that, *of course*, her grandmother would have zip ties handy.

"I had to go to the station to give a statement, but I told your grandmother which two doors you were planning to peek into today. She was pretty grim about it and didn't speak to me after that." Mark looked dejected. "I don't think she likes me, Lucy."

"You let me worry about her. She's going to love you. She doesn't really get a choice. Besides, she has her own shenanigans to answer for."

Lucy felt better, so they joined Gracie in the kitchen and helped carry everything outside. Mark lit some lanterns with candles scattered here and there and put a few small ones on the table for extra light. Lucy tasked him with grabbing the basket of throw blankets from the round reading room at the front of the house. She didn't want anyone leaving the conversation using the excuse of being cold.

Hattie pulled up—she'd gone home to change into warmer clothes—and set herself the task of getting everyone to the table. Sam was the only person missing. He'd gone home earlier because he wasn't feeling well after the news about Cami came through. Mark had promised to fill him in later about anything he needed to know.

Lucy looked around her. Many of the people she cared most about in the world were seated at the table, and for that, she was grateful. She planned to try to hold on to that feeling. After such a long and trying day, comfort food from Hattie's café seemed like just what they needed. Only Lucy pushed the food around on her plate more than eating. She didn't think she could relax until she'd heard the truth. *The whole truth and nothing but the truth,* she mentally added.

Mark updated everyone on what he'd learned from Andy. Cami was a student at the university where the professor was tenured in Valencia, Spain. But what they hadn't known was that Cami had convinced the professor to pose as her father and help her find what she believed was rightfully hers.

She'd written a paper and submitted it to the dissertation committee. However, they accused her of trying to commit fraud and wasting university time and resources. The only person on the committee who found her credible was Pedro Alvarez. Cami had swept him up in a tale of lost artifacts belonging to her family, believing they were stolen by knights and sequestered somewhere in the New World. He became more and more convinced that she was onto something and agreed to use his sabbatical to help her search for her family heirlooms. They settled on exploring the church first because she'd seen a picture of the stained-glass window and recognized it as a copy of one from a templar castle."

"How did Andy discover all this?" Lucy asked.

"They found the professor's notebooks in Cami's things. She'd packed up everything that could lead to the truth and was planning to flee the country, but Allen Morgan found her first. He killed the professor in the tunnels and later grabbed Cami and stashed her at a cabin in the woods. He'd run into the professor and tortured him to find out what he was looking for.

Allen already knew about the tunnels, and he knew something was hidden here in this house too."

"So that's why Allen was outside my tent the night Emma went missing? He was going to kidnap me and try to force me to take him to the treasure! But then poor Emma interrupted his plan." Lucy sent up a swift arrow of gratitude for Emma's safety.

"How did Allen know that?" Hattie asked, speaking just above a whisper. "Only a few of us knew."

"This is the part I wish I didn't have to tell you," Mark said. "Doctor Wilson has been arrested as an accomplice."

"What? No way!" Lucy was well and truly upset. "I think Andy must be letting the power go to his head again or something! That's just not possible. Dr. Wilson would never hurt any member of this family."

"Well, all I can tell you is that he did. He's the one who told Allen about the tunnels that connected to the sewer, and he's admitted telling him that there was treasure hidden here somewhere." Mark pressed his lips together, as if unwilling to say more.

"Why would he do that?" Lucy rubbed her eyes with the heels of her hand.

"I can think of only one reason," her grandpa said. "He must have been coerced. I'm going to guess that Allen threatened to harm his wife—Dr. Wilson's foster daughter. Doc and his wife love her as much as they do their boys."

"That's right. He threatened her and their children and had them stashed away too. He used that as leverage to get Dr. Wilson to spill what he knew." Mark sighed and dragged his fingers through his hair. "Andy thinks the charges against him will be reduced or dropped because he was acting under duress."

"Well, thankfully, he only knew a little. This is why we keep the circle small, Lucy. Harm can come to those who know. It can be used against them and against us."

"Mark, I think that's our cue to go." Hattie started to push her chair from the table. "The rest of this is a family matter."

Glo gave Hattie a tight smile and nod as thanks.

"Hold it! Mark and Hattie are my family. They are my family every bit as much as you are," Lucy said. "I want them to stay. If you want them to go, I'm going too, and you can take your precious secrets to the grave. You obviously don't trust me the way you should, but I'm your granddaughter, and you have to decide. Trust me to know who should be in my circle."

"Of course, we trust you, Lucy! We love you. We just want to protect you, honey." Her grandmother slapped the table. "I want to keep you safe, and if that means keeping you in the dark, then that's what I have to do."

"You're never going to keep me safe that way. All the secrets and all the lies, it's no way to live. It's time this family stopped being slaves to history. The past needs to stay in the past, and the future needs to be lived one hundred percent in the light of day." Lucy stared her grandmother down, refusing to blink.

"She's right, Glo. You know she's right." Her grandfather looked at Mark, who hadn't moved from Lucy's side, and Hattie, who was standing beside her chair. "Please stay. Lucy wants you here. I want you here." He turned to his wife. "Glo?"

"I just want you to know I've done my best, Lucy. I would never hurt you for anything. If you say Mark and Hattie are your family, then I agree. I've known Hattie my whole life, and she's never been anything but a true friend, even though we kept her in the dark, and she knew it. And Mark, well, all I need to know is written all over his face. He's not going anywhere, ever. Am I right?"

Mark nodded firmly—so firmly that she wondered if he'd given himself a tiny bit of whiplash. But she felt warm all the way through. She didn't want him to go anywhere, ever.

"Hattie, sit down. Stay for me." Lucy pleaded with her.

"I'll stay, but it's for all of you. I love each and every one of you, even this one." She pointed at Gracie. "You've only been here a short while, but I know your heart, and I've come to care about you a great deal. You're staying, right?"

Gracie smiled like the sun splitting the sky on a cloudy day. "I love you, too, Hattie. I am staying. But first, I think I'd better introduce myself."

"You all know me as Gracie, Graciela Jimenez. I've never been untruthful with any of you, and you need to know that Truth—with a capital T—is one of my core values. I've taken an oath to uphold and keep the truth. Some of you already know what I am about to tell you, and some of you will probably be up half the night searching online to see if what I said is true.

"I am Graciela Jimenez, and I grew up on the Iberian Peninsula with my father and uncles. My father was the last grand master of the Order of Montesa. The Order of Montesa has a long history and has its seat in the Kingdom of Aragon. Before the Order of Montesa was born, the Knights Templar were well-respected in the Kingdom of Aragon. So much so that every king entrusted them with their wealth and treasure.

"When the kingdoms were combined, a son of the Aragon branch entrusted the knights with the true Aragonese crown and the rose scepter of the kingdom to keep them from falling into the hands of the more powerful branches of the Castile family. There were legends about this crown and scepter, and their absence made the legends grow. It was said that the king who possessed the crown of Aragon and the rose scepter would be the true king of Spain.

"When the Vatican decided to destroy the Knights Templar, one group was spared from the pope's wrath: the knights of Aragon. They were found to be faithful and true and without any crime or stain. They disbanded, but the king sought permission to enact a new order, the Order of Montesa. He managed to populate the new order with many of the Knights Templar and left them to train and teach the new knights. They flourished, and the wealth of Aragon remained hidden from the Spanish kings as they consolidated more and more power.

"Finally, one king was more powerful than any other king in the history of Spain, and he was heir to the Holy Roman Empire that stretched through most of Europe, Asia, and parts of Africa. At one point, the Order of Montesa was tied to the throne, and the king automatically became the new grand master. That is how Phillip got his hands on the rose and crown. He was emperor and king of most of the world, even styling himself as king of the terra firma of the oceans and seas. He truly believed that God had consolidated all human authority and power and given it into his hands to rule. The so-called "divine right of kings" to rule was in no doubt to him. But then, in 1583, he had a medallion struck. On one side, it said, 'Philip II, King of Spain and the New World.' On the other, it said—"

Lucy cut in. "*Non sufficit orbis*. The world is not enough."

"That's right. When members of the order saw this, they worried. Phillip II was already the most powerful person on earth, and now he was determined to cement himself as the ruler of the New World too. He was only a hairsbreadth away from committing heresy and declaring himself divine when he declared that the world was not enough because only heaven was left to rule. He sent three ships filled with treasure to the New World to establish thrones for himself and his offspring to occupy.

"I do not know what became of the first two, which were supposedly sent to the East Coast of this country. The final ship was sent to the West Coast, and he planned to follow it at some later date and present himself to the world as the ruler of the New World. He sent a priest who was also a knight of the Order of Montesa to safeguard the treasure, but the brethren of the order were under great fear of divine judgment for such hubris. We believe that this knight hid the artifacts here for safekeeping.

"In the end, it didn't matter. Phillip was caught up with wars at home and abroad and never sailed for the New World. The legend of the rose and crown faded away, and the Order of Montesa held the only records of its transportation. I am one of the last and sworn to protect and safeguard the relics."

When Gracie stopped speaking, silence hovered over the table for several minutes. No one wanted to break the spell she'd woven of long-ago kings and kingdoms, of wealth, power, and ego. At last, Lucy spoke up.

"Are you going to take the rose and crown and medallion? Maybe they should be in a museum somewhere. It would probably not be a bad thing for this family to have one less secret to keep."

Ulyss smiled and shook his head. "No, Lucy-girl, she's not taking them. She's going to leave them where they are. Bearing this burden is our responsibility. We benefit, but we also pay the price.

Gracie made eye contact with everyone around the table. "I would like to leave them, yes. I could not do a better job of securing them myself. I plan to stay to help watch over them and divert any who may come looking. Cami descended from a cadet branch of the Castile family. There are those with long memories who passed legends and bitterness down through the generations. She had no claim but felt entitled. Others may feel the same. It's our job to make sure no head wears that crown and no hand holds that scepter—the last man who owned them nearly crowned himself the king of heaven and earth. Maybe it will be safe for them to come out of hiding in a few generations more."

Lucy stood up and went to her grandmother. "I'm sorry for giving you a hard time. I love you so much." She kissed Glo on the cheek and picked up her grandfather's hand. "I'd say this is our new circle, but Sam's not here. We'll have to give him the choice, but I know he'll want to be included." She walked around the table to Gracie and waited for her friend to stand up before giving her a hug. "Welcome to the family. If we have to keep this secret, we need to be a family. Only love can hold up under such a heavy burden."

"Si, soror, my sister. You are already in my heart."

Lucy came back around the table and hugged Hattie, whispering in her ear that she loved her.

Mark stood and walked over to Lucy, putting a strong arm around her shoulders. "Let's be a family then. All of us, but especially us." She understood the promise in his smiling eyes and said yes.

For the first time in her life, Lucy felt sure that she wasn't alone and that her life had a direction and a purpose. She felt what could only be called faith spring to life inside her. In the garden of her own making, filled with fairy lights and flowers, friends and family, she said yes. *Yes, to everything.*

Thank you

To my readers: Thank you for reading the second book in The Cozy Cat Bookstore Mysteries, *The Rose and Crown*. I hope you enjoyed reading it as much as I enjoyed writing it.

In case you were wondering, the town of Seaview doesn't exist on any California map, but you can find bits and pieces of it in places I love, such as Mendocino, Santa Cruz, and Carmel. If I were to add it to the map, I'd look for a spot somewhere on the central coast. I'm grateful for those places and the ones who introduced me to them.

I must also mention the inspiration for this series. His name is "The Great Catsby"—a noble and popular feline who runs a wonderful bookstore in the town of Mendocino. You can look him up online! I would be remiss not to mention the other great feline who helped me write this series. Her name is Muse, and she badly wishes to be credited as my co-author. That's the only reason I can think of for the following messages she hid within my manuscript. I think we rounded them all up, but you may attribute any typos you find to the cat. \\\\\\oO O-o \[p= \ [\';// ';'90 ';/-' Jk 8"""""""""""""" If anyone reads cat, please write to me and let me know what she said.

To my people: Without you, I'd be at a loss for words. Thank you. I love you each and every one.